THE TRUTH ABOUT CELIA

ALSO BY KEVIN BROCKMEIER

Things That Fall from the Sky
City of Names

THE TRUTH ABOUT CELIA

KEVIN BROCKMEIER

PANTHEON BOOKS, NEW YORK

All rights reserved under International and Pan-American Copyright
Conventions. Published in the United States by Pantheon Books,
a division of Random House, Inc., New York, and simultaneously
in Canada by Random House of Canada Limited, Toronto.

Pantheon Books and colophon are registered trademarks
of Random House, Inc.

Grateful acknowledgment is made to the following for permission
to reprint previously published material:
Far Corner Books: Poem "Over the Fence" from *Under the Words: Selected
Poems* by Naomi Shihab Nye. Copyright © 1995. Reprinted by
permission of Far Corner Books, Portland, Oregon.
Louisiana State University Press: Poem "Ghosts" from *Distractions: Poems*
by Miller Williams. Copyright © 1981 by Miller Williams. Reprinted by
permission of Louisiana State University Press.

Library of Congress Cataloging-in-Publication Data
Brockmeier, Kevin.
The truth about Celia / Kevin Brockmeier.
p.   cm.
ISBN 0-375-42135-1
1. Fantasy fiction—Authorship—Fiction. 2. Fathers and daughters—
Fiction. 3. Loss (Psychology)—Fiction. 4. Missing children—Fiction.
5. Girls—Fiction. I. Title.
PS3602.R63 T7 2003   813'.6—dc21   2002035513

www.pantheonbooks.com

Book design by Johanna S. Roebas

Printed in the United States of America
First Edition

2   4   6   8   9   7   5   3   1

The author—the real one—would like to thank his editor, Jenny Minton; his agent, Kyung Cho; the National Endowment for the Arts for financial support; and Meg Rains, Erin Ergenbright, and Meghan O'Rourke for early readings. There is a brief paraphrase of *The Book of the New Sun,* by Gene Wolfe, in the final section of *The Truth About Celia*.

the truth about

C e l i a

Christopher Brooks

Also by Christopher Brooks

Metaphysical Puzzleland

The Golden Age of Jumping (*stories*)

The Empty Space

Songs for Coming Out the Other Side (*stories*)

The Gates of Horn and Ivory Trilogy:
   The Mark of Abel
   The Cult of Beautiful Pain
   The Minutes

This book is dedicated to

Wednesday,

December 6, 1989.

So many years were stolen,
So many years are gone.
And the vision of my Celia
Made dreams to dream upon.
Each hour is a day filled with memories.
Oh, when will Celia come to me?

PHIL OCHS, "Celia"

Contents

A Note from the Author

The biographical note on the jacket of my last book reports that "Christopher Brooks is beginning work on a new novel, the projected sequel to his Gates of Horn and Ivory series."

This is not that book.

The stories in these pages were written after the disappearance of my daughter and after a long silence that, frankly, I did not expect to break. They are a mixture of fact and speculation, and of fact shading into speculation, and of speculation shading into fact. I think I believed that by writing them I could rescue or resurrect my daughter, that the fact might reconstruct her as she used to be and the speculation might call her back from wherever she is today. It is not the book I hoped it would be.

In any case, though I have drawn parts of it freely from my own imagination, many of the names, characters, settings, and events I employ are actual, and their resemblance to real events, places, and people, living or dead, is as exact as I could make it.

—CHRISTOPHER BROOKS

March 15, 1997

Here is Celia, running like a rabbit through the sunlight, on a day so perfectly pitched between winter and spring that she can feel streamers of warm air in the wind. The grass looks willowy and tender, and she very much wants to take off her shoes and flatten it beneath her feet, but her mom told her that if she went pounding around barefoot outside she might catch something. She is afraid of catching something. When she was six she caught the flu, and when she was five she caught the chicken pox. She stops by the pond and looks into the water, creased by the breeze. There is a cluster of minnows swimming just beneath the surface, and when she tries to touch one they scatter away in a spray of silver V's. Suddenly she thinks of a new jingle: *Little silver minnows with their little silver finnows*. It is a good day.

She has three favorite toys: her dollhouse, her ring collection, and her stuffed giraffe, Franklin, but they are all in her bedroom. Here in the yard there is only her scooter and the top half of a Barbie doll. The bottom half of the Barbie doll was washed away last week during a thunderstorm, when she and her parents had to walk through the house lighting tall white candles with matches as long as magicians' wands. It has been five days since it rained (one, two, three, four, five—she can count as high as one hundred), but the ground is still spongy in places. She leaves a deliberate curve of footprints across the backyard, stretching from the deck to the maple trees. She has known ever since she woke up this morning that something important was going to happen—something enormous—and though she does not yet know what it is, she can feel herself slowly falling toward it. It is like the dreamlike fall of a diver from a high board. Her fingers and toes are tingling. She does not need her toys.

She can see her dad through the kitchen window, escorting a man and woman past the pantry and the staircase and the wood-burning stove. I am her dad, and when I pass into the living room, she loses sight of me. In the pocket of her dress she finds a red rubber ball that she bought from the gum machine at the grocery store. Once a week her mom gives her a quarter to load into the gum machine, and though she always hopes for a plastic ring to add to her ring collection, usually she ends up cranking out a bracelet or a toy watch or something. She throws the ball as high as she can and it lands on the roof, drumming back down with a wonderful resiny thumping noise. Then she chases it across the grass and throws it once more, this time so high that it almost hits the chimney. She could listen to the sound it makes again and again, a hundred or a thousand times, but the fifth time she throws it, the ball lodges clunkily in the metal gutter. A great boat of a cloud drifts by. A dog barks across the street.

In one of the elm trees behind the house is a cocoon she has been watching all winter long, and though she has only touched it once or twice, as gently as she could, and with her littlest finger, when she looks for it she discovers that it has already split open. She is afraid to look inside. She can almost picture the body of the butterfly, motionless, folded into a papery kink. But the cocoon, it turns out, is empty, stuffed with a sticky gray floss that comes off on her fingers.

4

This means that the butterfly has flown away. Either that or been eaten.

She hasn't seen any butterflies swaying through the flowers yet this year, but she believes just the same, or decides to believe, that it has flown away.

Soon she is climbing onto the fragment of stone wall in the side yard of the house. The wall is almost as high as her waist, and she boosts herself onto it effortlessly. She can remember when she was little and had to scrabble to the top using both her hands and all her muscles. Her dad walks by the living room window and winks at her. She is tightrope-walking along the wall, her arms outstretched like wings, and just before he turns away, her hair is caught in the brilliance of the sunlight. He can see every individual thread. In less than a minute, now, the enormous thing she has been expecting all morning will carry her off like a wave. She watches a maple leaf, the last of the winter, go spinning delicately to the ground. She hears a car driving down the road, knuckles of asphalt popping in its wheel wells.

In her head she feels a rising sensation, like a halo of electricity traveling up a ring of conductors.

Three. Two. One.

It is the same day, two hours earlier, and I am looking through the closets and drawers in the house, weeding out items for our annual yard sale. A turtleneck sweater with a rippled weave. A letter opener in the shape of a sword. The yard sale is scheduled for next Saturday, the fourth weekend in March, as it was last year and the year before. We will, as it happens, postpone it this year and never reschedule it, and much later, after everything has changed, I will find a box labeled YARD SALE 1997 in the storage room, filled with all these forgotten objects, but I do not yet know this.

We have just come from the living room into the kitchen when Celia asks, "You're not going to give away the vegetable plates, are you?" She has been following me around the house all morning.

The vegetable plates are a set of eight plastic dishes with drawings of different vegetables on them—potatoes and carrots and the like. They all wear smiles on their faces, and Celia has an odd affection for them, as if they were pets. She has never explained it to me. "Not if you want us to keep them," I tell her. "And we're not *giving* anything away. We're *selling* things. It's a yard sale. Like the time we got Franklin, remember?"

And with that she's off, dancing around the room and waving her fingers like a baton: *Frank-lin. Meet my Frank-lin. He's a giraffe like you've never seen.* She has been doing this ever since she woke up—inventing jingles, one after the other.

"Honey, why don't you go look through your stuff? See if there's anything up there you want to get rid of."

"I looked yesterday and there wasn't any. But okay, Dad." She races upstairs, singing a new song, and when she rounds the corner, her voice dissolves away.

I have been Daddy to Celia for more than six years. It was her second word, right after Mommy and right before meatball (*mee-bah*), and it is only in the last few months that she has taken to calling me Dad. One syllable. Quick as a breath. She says it earnestly, almost primly, with a note of perfect self-command in her voice, and I can see that she is proud to be seven years old. There is never the same sloppy devotion in Dad that there was in Daddy, the same landslide of joy or sadness, but hearing it can still send me skipping forward through the rest of my day. And sometimes—this is my secret, and I keep it even from her— when I lay my hand on her forehead to test for a fever, or when I wake her from one of her cavernous midday naps, I will become Daddy again, for only a few minutes, until she takes possession of herself again.

Soon I hear her running back downstairs, leaping the last three steps.

"I *like* all my stuff," she says. "I don't *have* to give anything away, do I?"

"You don't have to, no," I say, "but I think you could do without—oh, say, your dollhouse."

"My dollhouse!" Her mouth opens in a circle—if a bee were to fly out, she could not look more surprised.

"That or your ring collection," I say. "You hardly ever play with those anymore."

She realizes I must be kidding, and she tests a smile. She begins another song, *Rings and things the mailman brings,* but stops short when she sees Janet.

Janet is my wife, her mother. She stands in the kitchen doorway gathering the tails of her wool muffler into her coat. "I'm off, kids," she says, tucking her clarinet case beneath her arm. On Saturdays she has Community Orchestra rehearsal, and she doesn't come back until two o'clock.

"It doesn't look that cold outside. Are you sure you want to wrap yourself up like that?"

"It'll be freezing in the Assembly Hall. Trust me. The priest over there likes to run the air conditioner even in January."

"All right," I say. "It's your sauna," and I kiss her goodbye.

She slips her hand into Celia's hair, making a spidery motion with her fingers. "You two take care of each other," she says. And I say, "We always do."

After she leaves, Celia and I return to our inventory of the kitchen, piling our yard-sale items into the same cardboard box I will one day find powdered with gray dust in the corner of the storage room. A Crock-Pot with a handle that has come unpinned on one side. A green ceramic saltcellar. An apron reading PLEASE DON'T FEED THE ANIMALS. Celia runs off to see what cartoons are on television, but comes back less than a minute later with the remote control in her hand. "Nothing but superheroes," she says. "I hate superheroes." Then she sings: *They can fly, through the sky, like a big pizza pie.*

I have finished sifting through the kitchen cabinets and ask her if she is ready for a break. "An ice cream break?" she says.

"We're out of ice cream, I think, but . . ."

When I open the freezer door, the cold comes sliding out in a single white sheet. You could almost imagine it dropping to the floor and shattering. I take a twin-pop from the popsicle box and line it up along the edge of the kitchen counter by the crease, knocking it into two halves with the heel of my palm. I give one half to Celia, and she shaves a curl of ice from it with her front teeth. The ice loses color as it lifts from the mass of the popsicle. This is something she likes to do: scrape popsicles down to the stick with her two front teeth. She takes a bite and asks, "So what room's next?"

I can feel the first throbs of a headache coming on, an edge-less few seconds of pain that vanishes almost as soon as it appears. Goddamn. I still have the library, the morning room, and the guest room to look through. "Next we go upstairs," I tell her. "We'll probably try the library first, and then—"

She belts out another jingle: *Oh, it's the books, books, books, books, books*—and my head gives a second twinge. A feather of plaster, as white as a snowflake, falls from the ceiling onto her shoulder. I brush it away.

"Tell you what, honey," I say. "Why don't you go play outside for a while?"

This time it happens differently. In my imagination it is always the same day—the sky is clear, the wind is fresh, and it happens again—but the details are never quite the same. Celia is running through the yard, chasing a speck of something that is glittering like a cinder in the sunlight. She can't quite see what it is—a housefly? A dandelion seed? All at once, it rises vertically in the wind and floats away over the roof of the house. She quits the chase. She wants to kick off her shoes and let the grass thread through her toes, feel the thin flexible edges bite ever so softly into her skin, but she does not. Instead she plays with the top half of her Barbie doll (the other half is missing) and throws her ball into the air and pokes at the minnows in the pond.

When she hears the sound of barking in the street, she thinks that it is Todd Paul Taulbee walking his two Irish setters. Todd Paul Taulbee is a friend of her dad's. He likes to fish in the pond behind their house, and he always lets her toss sticks to his dogs, who leap into the air and barrel after them, returning them to her in their slobbery black lips. She hurries into the front yard to pet the dogs and say hello, but as she rounds the corner she sees that it is not Todd Paul Taulbee after all. It is a tall, flat-haired man who stands in the street holding a sausage-shaped dog by the leash and staring at the house next door. His white-brown coat bulges enormously over his thin legs, which makes him look something like a mushroom.

Celia is not supposed to cross the street by herself, so she stops at the curb, calling, "What are you looking at?"

The man swings his head around, and his eyes run slowly down her face. It feels as though someone has cracked an egg over her head. "I'm friends with the girl who lives in that house," he says, pointing. "Do you know if she's home today?"

"You must be thinking of Beth Doyle. She moved away last year with her mom and dad."

"Beth Doyle, that's right." The man tugs on the leash and meets her at the curb, his dog pattering along at his feet.

"Why is your dog shaped like that?" Celia asks.

"That's just the way they come. They're called dachshunds." He stoops down to his ankles, massaging the dog's skull so that his lips are pulled back over his teeth. "His name's Teeter. You can stroke him if you want to."

When she bends over to pet him, the dog gives a bark and licks the back of her hand. His tongue feels smooth and flat, like wet paper, and his breath smells like glue. "Yuck," she says.

The man laughs—a thin, wheezing sound. "Lick him back. That's what I always do."

She can feel her mouth stretching into a grin. "No, you *don't*."

"No," he admits, and he winks at her. "I don't." A plastic bag, tangled in the hatching of a tree branch, balloons momentarily in the wind. She sees the hazy shape of her dad moving past the arched window of her bedroom, but he does not notice her. "What did you say your name was?" the man asks.

"Celia."

"Celia. Did you know that your tongue is purple, Celia?"

She extends her tongue, crossing her eyes to look at it, but sees only a lens-shaped slice of her own nose. "It must be from the popsicles. Purple is my favorite flavor."

"I'm feeling purple right about now myself," he says, and though she does not understand the joke, she laughs along with him. Her own favorite joke, ever since she was little, is a knock-knock joke: *Knock knock.—Who's there?—Banana.—Banana who?—Knock knock.—Who's there?—Banana.—Banana who?—Knock knock.—Who's there?—Orange.—Orange who?—Orange you glad I didn't say banana.* She likes the way the joke makes a perfect ring, wrapping around on itself again and again, like a pinwheel or a revolving door, but not everyone thinks it is funny. Sometimes she can lead her dad through four or five different bananas before he finally gives up on her.

"That's a wonderful joke," says the man with the sausage-shaped dog. "Did you come up with it all by yourself?"

"I don't think so."

"Well, it's a good joke anyway. Cute as can be."

Celia tries to think of a reply. "My mom says I'm cute as a bunny."

"Cute as a bunny, huh?" He taps her nose, letting his finger rest there for a second. "Wiggle, wiggle," he says, and his hand brushes over her face—first the cheek, then the lip. "Is your mom inside right now?"

"She's at rehearsal. My dad's inside, though. Do you want me to go get him?"

"No, no." A van drives down the road, jouncing noisily over a pothole, and pebbles of asphalt go spinning up into the carriage. The man, who has been crouching all this time, so that his enormous coat was draped over the curb, hiding his feet, and his eyes were level with her own, stands and softly takes her hand. "It's been a pleasure meeting you, Celia," he says. "I'll look for you—okay?"

The way he speaks makes it sound like a true question, and so she answers it. "Okay."

"Good." He squeezes her fingers, and she watches him walk up the street. A ripple of cloud passes over the sun, and a lawnmower buzzes from somewhere nearby. She tries to turn a cartwheel on the grass, but the ground is too wet, and she accidentally slides forward onto her elbows. She brushes herself off and then rinses her hands clean in the puddle by the chimney.

She does not see the man again for another half-hour, when she feels herself plunging off the fragment of stone wall between the two maple trees. We never find her.

Or maybe there was no man in a white-brown coat, no kidnapper who stole her away. It has been so long, and still we do not know. Sometimes, when I wake in the morning, floating upward through the last misty layers of sleep, I imagine I can see the world as she did that day. I watch her running through the yard in her blue jeans and sweater, kicking at the elm leaves in the grass. She kneels by the pond, her legs tucked beneath her in an X, and reaches for the minnows, and each time she does, her reflection crimps and separates on the surface of the water, until she no longer grabs for the minnows at all, just her own reflection, prodding and flicking at it. The tadpoles are easier to catch than the minnows, but they have not yet hatched this year. She pushes herself to her feet and races across the yard.

Her scooter is resting on its side beneath the deck. It is blue and white, with peeling red trim, and she takes its handle, settles her foot on the footboard, and propels herself around the house. The scooter trundles bumpily over all the little hills and troughs in the ground. It is harder to ride in the dirt and grass than it is on the pavement, but she is not allowed to play in the street without her mom or dad looking on. She is not allowed to stay up past nine o'clock, or eat snacks in her bedroom, or take her dollhouse to school with her. She is not allowed to do anything. She makes only one circle of the house before abandoning her scooter in the puddle behind the chimney, where a police detachment will find it later that evening.

The grass is soft and cushiony, green with rain, and she decides to lie down for a while. She props herself on her elbows and watches the pattern of shadows shift on the stone of the house. She can see her dad through the kitchen window, talking with a man and woman she does not know. I am her dad. The sunlight from the pond shimmers over her body in waves that look like golden wires. Her fingers tweeze a blade of grass into long, narrow threads. My God. When I cross into the living room, the window vanishes behind a wall and I lose sight of her.

The moisture from the grass is soaking through her blue jeans, and she pinches the fabric away from her skin. Then she stands and tromps to the edge of the yard. She winds through the elm trees behind the house, stopping beside her favorite. The cocoon that has been there since November is empty now, slit down the center, like a banana twisted at both its ends, and she can't help but feel disappointed. Once, last fall, she collected all the caterpillars she could find from the school play-ground, tens and twenties and thirties of them, peeling them off the bushes and dropping them into her lunch sack. On the way home she remembers stopping at a grocery store with her dad. The bag unfurled inside the car, and the caterpillars climbed free. By the time the two of them came back outside, the cater-pillars were everywhere: on the seats, the ceiling, the steering wheel. She had to collect them again and release them into the trees behind the house. By the next morning most of them were gone, but she did find one, spinning a pale, tight cocoon in the crutch of this branch. She sees a twitching high in the tree and thinks for a moment that it is the butterfly, but it is only the sprig of a leaf.

When the caterpillars escaped inside the car, her dad's face turned pale and smooth and he yelled at her. And this morning he yelled at her just for singing a song about the books in the library. She thinks for the hundredth time that she ought to run away. She could stay with her best friend Kristen Lanzetta, or her other friend Oscar Martin, or she could sleep on the gym mats at school. If she left home and did not come back for five days (she can count as high as one hundred), then her mom and dad would have to be nice to her.

She presses a line of footprints into the ground, which is still spongy from the big storm, stamping every time her foot falls and slowly rolling her weight to make each step sharp and deep. When she has finished, she sits on the fragment of stone wall and lets her eyes follow the trail she has made. She feels like a hunter or a detective, so easily able to trace where she has been. Though she is not supposed to remove her shoes outside, she decides to take them off anyway, burrowing her feet into the cool black dirt. She is not wearing any socks, and she pretends her toes are earthworms. She shivers and laces her shoes back onto her feet. She is afraid of catching something.

As she balances herself atop the stone wall, extending her arms and placing one foot in front of the other like an acrobat, her dad walks past the living room window and looks out at her. He winks at her, but she pretends not to notice him. For no good reason, he sent her outside when he was gathering stuff for the yard sale. A yard sale is when you set tables and boxes up in the front yard and let people take your things away. She likes all her things and wishes that she could keep them, but didn't her dad say that she would have to give her stuffed giraffe away? She feels a prickling heat behind her eyes and blinks a few times to keep from crying.

A maple leaf skates across the tips of the grass.

A dog barks repeatedly across the street.

She can picture her dad opening her bedroom door, spreading his arms wide, and telling the man and woman she does not know that they can help themselves, take anything they want, feel free to look around. She leaps from the wall and begins to run.

"Tell you what, Celia," I say. "Why don't you go outside and play?"

It is an hour earlier, and we are finishing our popsicles, biting the last clumps of ice, which have already melted to sleet, from around the center of the stick. She presses hers against the roof of her mouth, and I hear her breath puffing flatly through her nose. This is something else she does: breathes through her nose whenever she chews or swallows. At its loudest, when she has a cold, it reminds me of the sound that air makes escaping from a balloon. "Now?" she asks.

"Just for a little while. Is your sweater in your bedroom? You should probably go put it on."

"*O*-kay," she says. Two notes. She snaps her popsicle stick in half, drops it in the trash, and ascends the stairs.

I decide to take a Tylenol for my headache and so am in the bathroom when she leaves.

It is another half hour, and I have finished my inspection of both the library and the guest room, when I hear a knock on the front door. Our house is an old one, listed in the State Registry of Historic Places, with a stone fireplace, a winding wooden staircase, and a pantry as large as the kitchen. One Saturday a month I conduct any visitors who come to the door through its rooms, recounting the story of its construction, which I know by heart. Today the visitors are Donald and Joan Pytlik, who are traveling across the region in their minivan to visit all the houses catalogued in the State Department of Recreation and Tourism brochure. It wasn't them.

"We had been wanting to take this trip for twenty years, but there never seemed to be the time," Mrs. Pytlik says, draping her jacket over the coat-frame in the hall.

"So we *made* the time," Mr. Pytlik says. He shifts his leather belt around his large belly.

They stand by the door, holding hands.

"Your house is certainly beautiful," says Mrs. Pytlik, and Mr. Pytlik says, "It is, it is," and I thank them. Then I lead them into the front room and begin my recitation.

I show them the rounded baseboards and the antique glass table and the fireplace with the ash-darkened hearth. I show them the hatch in the wall that used to lead to the coal cellar. There is a corner of the pantry where the wood is a slightly darker shade of brown, and I tell them how we had to replace a few boards when a mysterious rot began to spread through them in 1995. In the kitchen I show them the wood-burning stove, which has been in place since the house was constructed in the mid-1800s. "But we rarely use it," I say. "After all, we have the fireplace to heat the living room and the gas oven to cook our food." I can see Celia through the kitchen window, playing safely in the backyard. "Not to mention central heating and the microwave," I finish, and I usher the Pytliks into the living room. Beneath the winding staircase, carved from a single giant sycamore, I point to the place where the woodwright incised his name some hundred and fifty years ago—Edwin Reasoner. I let them trace it with their fingers. This is how I conduct my tour, every third Saturday of the month.

We are upstairs in the master bedroom when we hear a thump on the roof, followed by a drumming noise which accelerates and comes to a sudden stop. It sounds like a bullet of hail, but the sky is perfectly blue.

"What on earth was that?" Mrs. Pytlik says, her hands on her hips, staring at the ceiling.

"A bird must have dropped something," her husband says.

"Or something dropped a bird," she says.

There is another crack above us, slightly louder this time, and their shoulders give a start.

I can still hear Celia galloping around in the backyard, and

I am not concerned. "Nothing to worry about. Now if you'd like to follow me down the hall, I can show you the morning room." We hear the sound three more times before it stops, with a tinny clank.

Later, as I escort the Pytliks back downstairs, the phone begins to ring, and I answer it in the kitchen. It is Janet, on recess from her session with the Community Orchestra. "They're rehearsing the strings right now," she says. "Listen, I'm going to stop by the grocery store on the way home. Do we need anything?"

"Hamburger buns. And paper towels. And I think Celia just lost her last rubber ball, so—"

"—so whatever I do, don't buy another."

"Exactly."

She laughs. "Are you guys okay?"

"We're fine. Celia's playing outside. I'm showing the house to a couple from upstate."

"Oh! I'll let you go, then." She blows a kiss into the transmitter—a chirping sound. "Take care," she says.

I return the telephone to its cradle.

The Pytliks are waiting for me in the living room, looking at the photographs framed on the mantelpiece. I step over to the window and stand there for a moment. Celia is tightrope-walking along the fragment of stone wall between the two maple trees. Her arms are open wide, and she steps delicately, the way a leaf falls, from the shadow of the trees into the sunlight. I catch her gaze and wink at her. I want to understand what she is thinking, in this moment just before it happens (though I do not yet know that it will happen). What is she remembering, or noticing, or imagining? What is she watching so intently? It is important to me. Watching her, I feel an enormous plummeting sensation in my legs, as if I have missed the last step on a ladder, though it may be that I feel this only in retrospect. I do not know.

Behind me Mrs. Pytlik clears her throat, and I hear the rustle of her skirt shifting on her body. "So where did the stone for the outside walls come from?" she asks. And I turn away.

It goes on happening.

Celia is running through the grass, as fast as she possibly can, and the arms and legs of her shadow are scissoring back and forth beneath her feet. It is almost noon. The way the sunlight flickers inside the branches of the trees reminds her of the flashing siren of an ambulance or a police car, and when she comes kicking to a stop, she gulps in air and blinks her eyes to see if she can duplicate the effect. The house vanishes and reappears, and so does the sky, and so does the ground. At school, during Career Day, a doctor visited her class with an ambulance, a policeman with a police car, and a fireman with a fire truck. They all ran their sirens simultaneously when one of the boys, Oscar Martin, asked them to, and it was so loud that she had to clap her hands over her ears. She climbs onto the deck and looks down at the yard, where the wind is making patterns in the grass, little pleats and ripples. She thinks of another jingle: *All of the grass and all of the wind, oh they couldn't put Humpty together again.*

A plastic bag, the kind you get from the grocery store, is tangled in the twigs of the tree beside the chimney, and she can see it rustling every time the breeze shifts. The tree is an elm tree, but her mom calls it the Plastic Bag Tree, because every few days another plastic bag will appear there like a tattered blue or white flower. Her dad has to pull them loose with a long hook. He says that it must have something to do with the air currents.

She climbs down from the deck, jumping at the fifth stair from the bottom, and lands with a flat smack of her sneakers. A lawnmower buzzes across the street. The minnows in the pond glitter like silver nickels. There are flags of warm air in the wind. She can tell that spring is almost here. The next holiday on the calendar is Easter, and the last was St. Valentine's Day.

When she boosts herself onto the stone wall, she sees a spider concealing itself in one of the cracks, so thin a brown that it is almost transparent, but she is not frightened of spiders. She sits and pulls her knees to her chin, then tightens her shoelaces. A chip of yellow rock zings away when she knocks her foot against the side of the wall. She rises and spreads her arms and paces along the ledge to the other end, where the wall crumbles into a staircase of dented stones, and then she sits down again. Out of the corner of her eye she sees something moving.

There it is. The butterfly.

It has settled on the border of the very last stone and is swaying gently in the breeze. She watches it close its wings. They fold together, meet in a plane, and then, to her surprise, fold closer still, crossing into one another, so that she cannot see the butterfly at all anymore. It is as though it has simply hidden itself away in the spaces between the air. She wonders if it has melted to nothing, like a puff of fog, but then the wings swivel back into sight and it is resting right where it was before. She wipes her eyes and looks more closely. Its antennae give a few twitches. It lifts one of its legs. A moment later she watches it happen all over again: first it is there and then it is gone.

It is like nothing she has ever seen before, and when the butterfly opens its wings again, dipping and tilting its head, she reaches out to take it in her hand.

Faces, and How They
Look from Behind

The pavilion where United States Congressman Asa Hutchinson sleeps was built in 1989, the year he finally gave up on the world. George Bush was president at the time, and then Bill Clinton, and then George Bush again, but a different George Bush, a younger one. The congressman lives in the pavilion every year from May to October, when he hitchhikes north, into the winter. He knows the exact path the squirrels follow when crossing the rafters, and he can hear the lapping waters of the reservoir even when he plugs his ears, the way that roller skaters will feel their legs gliding beneath them long after they have removed their skates. The Community Orchestra uses the pavilion as a concert shell on Memorial Day, but the one year they tried to remove Congressman Hutchinson—1995—he cried out that he was being kidnapped, flailing his limbs so wildly that he broke the first violinist's nose, and they allow him to listen now from his bench in the corner. He applauds, loudly, at every silence and weeps openly into his hands. He seems to think they are generating the music just for him. The congressman spends hours every day asking passers-by if they can spare a dollar, a quarter, a nickel, some change, which is what he asks as Tommy Taulbee jogs past the pavilion this morning. Asa Hutchinson has never heard of the actual United States Congressman Asa Hutchinson, who rose to prominence during the Whitewater hearings and later directed the DEA. The fact that people suddenly began calling him Congressman one year, with a knowing grin, and later by simple routine, he considers, like so many other things, beyond explanation.

Tommy Taulbee tosses a quarter to the congressman as he huffs through the park, flipping it off his thumb and forefinger so that it looks like a perfect, spinning globe. Every day Tommy jogs two miles along the reservoir before he showers and drives to school. He teaches four sections of senior English at Springfield High School, with the first two periods of his day reserved for prep, so that he doesn't actually have to appear in his classroom until ten-fifteen. From May to October he sets out on his jog with a quarter already tucked in his hand, and when he tosses it to Congressman Asa Hutchinson, the congressman always says that he thanks him for his goodness and mercy, which have followed him all the days of his life. On those few mornings when the congressman has wandered away from the park, Tommy arrives home with the quarter still in his hand, its ridges incised neatly into his palm. He runs past the empty public playground, the brewery, and the T-shaped docks with their chains of boats, thinking about all the papers he has yet to grade. Yesterday one of his students, Pierre Douglas, turned in an essay making the argument that people with guns should not shoot bystanders. Another, Chrissy Symancyk, wrote a science-fiction story that ended with the heroine, Chrissy herself, waking in what she called *a poodle of sweat.* He likes his students, even admires many of them, but when he returns their papers he often has to prevent a note of ridicule from puckering his voice. He listens to his tennis shoes slapping the pavement as he crosses the street—they echo off the broad side of a building with a surprisingly explosive series of cracks. It is a beautiful, still morning, cool and sunny, with hardly a breath of wind in the air. Tommy jogs past the Why Not Bar and the Lily Taylor Hair Salon and the Quik Stop Convenience Store, where

Christopher Brooks stands at the counter, buying a bottle of eyedrops and a box of antacids. Christopher watches him pass.

He pays for the eyedrops and the antacids with a five-dollar bill, pocketing the change, and grips the bell hanging from the door as he leaves, muffling it in his hand so that it won't jingle. This is something he has found himself doing these past few years, and he does not know why. The doors at the newer shops and convenience stores, with their electronic chimes that ding automatically, make him ever so fractionally uncomfortable, and he can feel his face wincing whenever he goes to open one. As he heads down the sidewalk toward his car, his stomach sends a sudden, liquid pain through his body that causes his toes to tighten and a terrible heat to roll through the soles of his feet. It feels as though something inside him is wobbling just at the point of collapse, like a bead of water immediately before it spills out of itself. He is a mess. He stops by the door of the Why Not Bar, pressing his hand to his gut, and waits for the sensation to crest and fade away. Rollie Onopa calls out to him from the roof, where he is replacing a line of rain-rotted shingles. He says that he and the wife and the daughter will be there this evening for sure, they wouldn't miss it, he just wants to let Christopher know, and Christopher says that he appreciates it. I'll see you later on tonight, then, Christopher calls to him, and Rollie says, You can count on it.

Rollie takes another few nails from the box as Christopher swallows his breath and pushes on toward the car. He squares one beneath the hammer and holds the other three in his mouth like toothpicks. Since there are no more joggers on the street, he knocks the nail into the shingle with a gentle tap, then drives it through with one easy swing. He takes a clean muscular pride in his facility with tools, in sawing smoothly through the kinks in a block of wood or whipping a spare lump of mortar off his trowel. He remembers his father telling him that the best men in the world knew how to use a tool, that Jesus Himself was a carpenter and you can be damn sure that when He fixed the joint in a door, that joint was by God perfect. Whenever Rollie spots joggers running below him, he likes to hammer in time with their footfalls. The way they stare at their feet trying to figure out what's going on always amuses him. He certainly confused the hell out of the one who passed a few minutes ago, that schoolteacher. He lays another shingle on the roof. His daughter means everything to him, and he doesn't know what he would do if he were to lose her. He can't imagine how Christopher manages to get out of bed in the morning, to drive into town, to buy eyedrops and envelopes as though nothing has happened. After he has nailed the shingle in place, he stands and stretches into the sunlight, a single pearl of sweat sliding down his back. From the roof of the bar the road through town looks like an ascending chain of stoplights, falling green one by one, and just before he bends to his knees again he sees Christopher's car disappearing over the brow of the hill.

The traffic is light, and Christopher drives home as quickly as he can. A Styrofoam cup stirs and lifts behind a schoolbus, tumbling over his hood, and he watches it sail smartly into a telephone pole. He is preparing himself for his daughter's memorial service. When he gets home he takes a pair of the antacids he bought, washing them down with a glass of ginger ale, which a school nurse once told him was good for soothing the stomach. He does not believe that Celia is dead. He does not even believe that she is not coming back. She simply vanished one day, when she was seven years old, and they have not been able to find her. *Little Bo Peep has lost her sheep and doesn't know where to find them.* When she was a toddler, this was her favorite nursery rhyme. Christopher used to recite it to her every night before she went to sleep, leaning over her bed's protective railing to kiss her good night. Lately he hears its bobbing cadence in his head a dozen times a day. He has even begun to match his stride to it. His wife, Janet, is upstairs in their bedroom sifting through the closet, and the sound of the wire hangers scraping along the metal rod, the empty ones tinkling loosely together, sounds to him like a wind chime combined with a rotary saw. The memorial service was Janet's idea. Several weeks ago the two of them were having an argument about books that became an argument about Celia that became an argument about when he was going to climb free of it. He does not believe that he will ever climb free of it. He is not ready to memorialize his daughter, or at least he is not ready to ceremonialize her: in his own way he has been memorializing her ever since she was born. When she was three she swallowed a button. When she was five she climbed a maple tree. When she was six she found a yellow jacket in her room, but she wouldn't let him kill it. He had to capture it in a butter dish and set it free outside. He is standing in the living room, staring blankly out the window.

Janet does not know which dress to wear to the service. She has inspected all of them, draping them over her body with the collar pinned under her chin and the sleeves trailing down her arms so that she looks in the mirror like a statue of Saint Francis blessing the animals. She has looked at each dress more than once—so many times, in fact, that they have become just so much fabric to her, a great illimitable ocean of fabric—and she is sitting on the floor now, paddling her hand through them like Celia used to do when she crawled beneath the carousels at the department store. She owns only two black dresses, both of them of the sexy little number variety, and while she would love to wear simply her blue jeans, softened to velvet from years of laundering, she knows that she cannot. She hears Christopher downstairs, shuffling into the kitchen and rinsing something out in the sink. It was only two weeks ago when he told her that the only reason she didn't like James Agee's *A Death in the Family* was that she couldn't stand to believe that the world was sad, and she told him that the only reason he didn't like John Fowles's *The Magus* was that he couldn't stand to believe that the world was meaningless, and he said, But the world *is* sad, and she said, But the world *is* meaningless, or at least it can be, Christopher, and then somehow she ended up insisting that it was time to have a funeral—it had been four years, after all, it was something she needed, and if he wasn't ready for a funeral, then surely he could allow her a simple memorial service, was that too much to ask? When the phone rings, she is briefly startled, as though someone has suddenly appeared in the room screaming. She does not remember when she began flinching at the sound of doorbells and telephones, at all the familiar announcements of company, only that she was different once, a few years ago. She answers the phone to the voice of Reverend Gautreaux, who says that he is just calling to see if she is ready for the ceremony tonight and to ask how she is holding up, but he has no advice to offer when she says that she can't seem to find a proper dress.

The Reverend tamps a cigarette quietly against his wristwatch, flexing his toes in the cool deep carpet of the vestry. He tells Janet that if there is nothing else, he will see her this evening at the pavilion, the weather should be lovely, and if she needs any last-minute help before then, she can always find him here at the church. I should be okay until tonight, she says, and he tells her, Well, just in case, then. . . . After he hangs up, he lights his cigarette, smoking it quickly, furtively, and then lights and smokes a second one. He has told his new assistant, Miss Unwer, that he has already quit smoking, and he allows himself to hope, though never to pray, that he will finish before she discovers him. He has hidden a palm-sized fan in the wardrobe to loosen and disperse the smoke, but when he turns it on, it makes the angry, granular whine of a horsefly, and he does not like to use it. He can see the smoke hovering over him in a thin fog. He will be offering the eulogy tonight. He is a young man, only twenty-nine, barely out of seminary, and this is his first congregation. He notches his lighter into the empty cigarette packet and conceals it in a small inner drawer of the wardrobe atop a neat stack of other cigarette packets. He has two secrets, the lesser of which is his smoking habit, and the greater of which is this: he has been unable to pray these last few months, ever since his father died. He feels sometimes that he has become one of the damned, those to whom prayer is forbidden. He slips his shoes on and opens the vestry door and steps out into the sanctuary. His father spent his entire life trying to read the Bible from cover to cover, and when he died, at sixty, of a heart attack, the Reverend Gautreaux found his bookmark six pages from the last amen, at the eighteenth chapter of the Book of Revelation. He does not understand how a life could end so abruptly, so close to its natural completion.

The Reverend hears a premonitory cough in the pews and turns to see Kimson Perry, the police chief, standing there with his arms crossed. Kimson asks him how his smoke was and then laughs at the way his face blanches. The Reverend is so easy to rattle that Kimson can't help himself sometimes. The sun shining through the stained-glass window casts an arrowhead of red and yellow light down the aisle, and Kimson follows it to the chancel. He likes to call the Reverend *Rev*, filling the smile that always spreads out from his lips with the sound of a revving engine. He was the first officer to investigate the disappearance of the little girl, the Brookses' daughter. The Reverend looks at his watch and tells Kimson that he's about an hour early for the noon mass, which is a joke. Kimson is a determined agnostic. The Reverend likes to tell him that this is exactly right, he is downright *determined* not to know, to which Kimson always answers, No, I'm determined not to *pretend* that I know. Kimson says that he has come to ask the Reverend if he wants to catch an early lunch, before the flock comes calling, and the Reverend nods and feels behind him for his wallet. He calls out to Miss Unwer that he is leaving for half an hour, then tells Kimson to lead the way. Kimson knows that the Reverend considers his agnosticism a form of intellectual laziness, and he likes to debate the matter with him once or twice a week over lunch. It is Kimson's thought that the Reverend thinks of life as a dart, which is to say that what matters to him is where it will land, while Kimson himself thinks of life as a paper airplane, which is to say that what matters is the fact that it's flying. He has been waiting to use this metaphor for almost a month, but the Reverend has seemed dispirited lately, as if Kimson could poke right through their banter and find him shriveled to his bones with anxiety. He has had to ease away from the debate. A ruff of clouds hangs just around the sun, like a tire. On their way to the diner, Kimson and the Reverend have to step off the sidewalk to weave past Enid Embry, who is carrying a swaying tower of Tupperware to her car—meat loaf tubs and picnic hampers and soup tureens.

Enid Embry lifts the door handle with the very tips of her fingers, probing blindly, and totters around the edge of the door as she opens it, allowing the Tupperware to tumble willy-nilly into her backseat. Ever since her husband retired and passed away—God rest his soul—she has spent her days baking for her friends and neighbors and listening to broadcasts of *The Art Bell Show*. One thing she has discovered is that even her dearest friends often do not return her Tupperware, so once a year she orders a completely new set, picking it up from Belinda Kuperman, her Tupperware agent, in four separate shipments. Enid lives directly across the street from the Brooks family—though can she really call them a family anymore, now that it is just the two of them? She doesn't know. After she has driven home, she bakes a pan of Macaroni Hot Dog Surprise and waits for it to cool on the counter. Art Bell is discussing time travel with his callers: Is time travel possible? How would a time traveler avoid the infamous temporal paradoxes popularized by *Star Trek* and the *Back to the Future* movies? The air in Enid's kitchen is thickening with the scent of cheese and hot dogs and a hint of nutmeg, which is the Surprise in her Macaroni Hot Dog Surprise. Enid has seen three flying saucers in her life—wavering silver brightnesses that paused over her house and then lifted suddenly away—though two of them were actually cigar-shaped. One of the callers informs Art Bell that he is himself a time traveler, but when Mr. Bell asks the caller what the coming decade holds in store for us, the caller will say only that there will be a war somewhere, and an earthquake somewhere else, and that a beloved Hollywood film star will die. After the Macaroni Hot Dog Surprise has cooled, Enid slides it out of the pan, listening to the heavy wet kissing noise it makes as she levers it free with a spatula, then she seals it in a Tupperware container. She carries it outside and across the street.

Janet answers the door to that woman from across the way, Enid Embry, the one who has referred to her and Christopher as *You Poor People* ever since Celia went missing. I brought *You Poor People* something to eat. If *You Poor People* need anything, don't hesitate to call on me. Janet can't help but grate her teeth when she hears the phrase, biting so hard that she thinks sometimes they will shear apart like pieces of shale, but she knows that Enid means well, and she thanks her for the Macaroni Hot Dog Surprise. Enid says goodbye, and Janet shuts the door. There is a small breeze in the air that was not there this morning, and she can feel it pushing through the open kitchen window, swelling every so often and rattling the cooking utensils that hang on their metal hooks. She picks up an envelope that has wafted to the floor—a royalty check from Christopher's publisher. Thank God the old books are still selling. He hasn't been able to write anything in years. She has decided that she will have to buy a new dress for the funeral—or, rather, for the memorial service. Though she has reminded Christopher of the distinction a thousand times, she still finds herself making the same slip in her innermost thoughts. She discovers him in the bathroom, where he is standing with his head craned back, his mouth open in a hapless O, squeezing eyedrops into his eyes. He looks almost like a baby bird begging for food, so adorably helpless that she can't help but forgive him for a moment for everything he's ever done, laughing and kissing him on the cheek. She tells him that she is going to head into town for a while. Do you need anything? she asks, and he says that he doesn't, futilely trying to smother a yawn.

The impulse is irresistible: whenever Christopher tilts his head back and stares into the light, the yawns rise through him one after another, entire chains of them, as though he were simply a chimney exhaling rings of smoke. Janet heads upstairs in her socks, and a few minutes later he hears her marching back down, her footsteps sounding more square and solid in her shoes. He switches the bathroom light off. It has been weeks since he slept through till morning, and yesterday, when he was shaving, he found a tick-sized system of exploded blood vessels in his right eye. Every night he wakes at two or three o'clock, when even the frogs and the crickets have fallen silent. No matter what he tries he can't settle back to sleep. He pads to the kitchen in his T-shirt and underwear and eats boluses of peanut butter from the end of a spoon, plates of leftover casserole, entire boxes of saltine crackers. Once, at four in the morning, Janet stumbled into the kitchen and caught him with a brick of cheddar in one hand and a cucumber in the other, both cheeks bloated with food, and she turned around and went back to bed. He has learned what every beggar knows: that for short periods of time, a few days perhaps, no longer, he can replace sleep with eating or eating with sleep, though it has been at least twenty-four hours since he has done either. His stomach is just now beginning to settle. The last time he saw Celia she was balancing herself on the stone wall in the side yard of their house, the arms of a maple tree stretching above her. This was through his living room window, and when he looked again, a few minutes later, she was gone. Janet calls goodbye to him from the foyer, closing the front door just as he closes the kitchen window, and the air, which had been flowing past him in loops and curves, seems to tighten suddenly and take on the shape of the room.

It is a lovely day, the sky so powdery blue that Janet almost decides to walk to the store, but she would rather not have to carry her outfit back home. She drives into town with all four windows open, parking by the reservoir. D. Barnett Fashions, where she is planning to buy her dress, is less than a block away, just past the Quik Stop Convenience Store and the Lily Taylor Hair Salon and the Why Not Bar, which Rollie Onopa, the proprietor, named from a line in a song. The wind carries the rich sweet smell of the first browning leaves, a smell that has always reminded her of burnt marshmallows. When she was a child, she used to roast marshmallows in the fireplace every Christmas Eve while she and her parents watched *Rudolph the Red-Nosed Reindeer* on TV. On the Christmas after Celia's seventh birthday, a few short months before she vanished, Janet and Christopher gave her a Barbie doll and a set of glitter lipstick. It occurs to Janet that she would love to go to a movie this afternoon, to seal herself in a dark room for an hour and a half, completely anonymous, immersing all her sorrow and passion and curiosity in someone else's story, a fiction, and then to step outside and clutch her chest and rock back on her heels, blindsided by the fresh air and sunlight. She is no longer welcome at the Reservoir Ten, where she tore one of the movie screens a year or two ago—a long story—but she could easily visit one of the other theaters in town. She does not have the time, though. She would not be able to concentrate. And anyway she has to buy a dress. She is passing the pavilion where United States Congressman Asa Hutchinson stands asking for a quarter, a dollar, anything you can spare, when she sees Sheila Lanzetta, whose daughter, Kristen, was Celia's best friend, sitting at a picnic table paging through a journal.

Sheila hears someone tapping past her on the sidewalk. She is reading an article in the latest issue of *Social Text*, a long, tangled piece about aboriginal Filipino culture and the concept of feminine time, a term the author uses without attribution, as though she has coined it. The author's argument relies heavily on the ideas of Baudrillard and Kristeva, writers whose work has always seemed just so much wet cement to Sheila, and she has spent the last half hour or so trying to puzzle out the connection between multiple refractivity and the hermeneutics of the feminine. As such, she almost fails to see the person passing by, barely glancing up from her reading. Janet's face is turned fully away from her, toward the sunlight crinkling on the surface of the reservoir, but Sheila recognizes her from the way she carries herself, her hands curled loosely into fists like a person holding a firefly she is trying not to crush. When Sheila calls out to her, Janet stops and spins about, a little too surprised, and gives a tiny laugh. She says that she was lost in her thoughts and didn't see her. Sheila smiles. You were hoping I wouldn't spot you, right? she asks, and Janet grimaces and admits that, yes, she was. She says that she has so many things on her mind right now, you know how it is, and Sheila says that she can certainly sympathize. Ever since Janet lost her daughter, she has fallen into uncomfortable languishing silences around Sheila, and Sheila believes that she understands why: it has to do with watching Kristen grow up and take on the first features of her adolescence, pierced ears and braces and training bras. Janet must see her own daughter, or what she could have been, reflected there. A page of Sheila's journal, pressed open on the picnic table, lifts in the wind and then turns over, sagging down on itself. She can see that she is keeping Janet waiting, and so she tells her that she and Tim will see her tonight at the service. And Kristen will be there, too, if we can convince her to come, she says. Janet nods goodbye, and Sheila watches her stop for only a moment as she walks away, fishing a dollar out of her purse for United States Congressman Asa Hutchinson.

Congressman Hutchinson folds the bill into quarters, tucking it into the change pocket he has sewn into the band of his pants. He can tell by the way the pocket weighs against his gut that he will soon have enough for a drink of liquor. Empty bottles are stacked three deep along the rafter above his bench, and he can hear them clinking whenever a gust of wind shakes the pavilion. Once he made the mistake of telling a woman, a Jehovah's Witness, that the dollar she had given him was the last he needed for the day and that now he was going to get good and drunk. He had reached out to shake her hand, saying what he always said when his pocket was finally full or he had generated enough warmth beneath his blanket to fall asleep, when, in short, any good thing happened to him, The Lord is my shepherd, I shall not want, The Lord is my shepherd, I shall not want, and the woman had demanded her money back. This was in another city, in the winter, when he was traveling. A bluebird flutters past him and perches on the white railing of the stairs, excavating something from its feathers. It is September now, and he knows he will have to leave soon. Every year from November to April he tends his wife's grave, combing the leaves from the grass and digging it free of the ice and snow. It is the least he can do for her. The groundskeeper of the cemetery knows him so well that he allows him to borrow his rake and shovel. The congressman's wife fell sick with cancer in 1989— the same year that Celia was born, the same year the pavilion was built. Before she died, she made him promise to look after her burial plot in the winter. She said that she couldn't stand the thought of being covered by all that snow. The congressman has groomed the site so many times by now that he has memorized the boundary line, and when he returns the groundskeeper's rake and shovel to him, he leaves behind a perfect rectangle of yellowing grass. A squirrel crosses the rafters above his head, running first around the periphery and then along one of the spokes. It pauses halfway down a column to leap onto the trunk of an oak tree, scrabbling into the branches. The congressman watches it twist out of sight toward the Quik Stop and the liquor store as he gives his change pocket a protective tap.

If you are small enough and nimble enough, the trees are like a system of roads, and before half a minute has passed the squirrel has leaped from one tree onto another, and from that tree onto a third, leaving the sour smell of the pavilion far behind. There was a time, not fifty years ago, when you could cross the entire town without ever touching ground. The trees might have fallen, but the houses and strip malls and street-lamps have risen, and the squirrel sometimes races along them for miles, running as though he could never fall. He darts from a rooftop onto a fence, and from there onto a tree and a bill-board. When he reaches the west end of town, the interlacing canopies of the trees take him across entire yards, and occasionally two or three branches will even meet above a busy street. He runs through the elm trees behind a row of apartments and crawls to the very tip of a branch that stretches far into the open air, testing the pliancy of the limb with his paw, then jumps onto a windowsill, allowing the spring of the bough to propel him a few extra inches. A few clusters of birds are pecking up bread crumbs from the grass, and when he bounds into the midst of them, the birds scatter and beat their way into the air—an exhilarating noise. He climbs over a wire fence and into a spindly cherry tree with a few red leaves still curling open inside it. It is almost autumn. He is biting into a wild cherry, gnawing around the hard, blackened dimple at one end, when he hears a sudden pop and a chip of bark flies into his side. He lights out.

Pierre Douglas doesn't even see where the damned squirrel goes, only a flash of its tail and a twitching in the leaves. He rests the stock of the gun against his shoe, squinting into the sunlight. The wind is blowing in hard gusts from behind him, and because the elastic bands keep vanishing from his bathroom counter, he has to hold his hair out of his face with his hand. His girlfriend, Claire, wants him to wear his hair like he did when they first started dating, loose and scrappy like Thurston Moore from Sonic Youth, but he likes it better when it's fastened into a ponytail. He hardly listens to Sonic Youth anymore. Lately he's been getting into Tom Waits and the early Van Morrison. When he opens the back door, standing the gun against the wall, he can hear Claire singing "Mary Had a Little Lamb" to their son Pierre, the only song that will put him to sleep this early in the day. Claire calls the boy Pierre Jr., but

Pierre himself likes to call him Pierre the Second—it makes him sound like royalty, he thinks, like a king, or maybe a pope. He finds Claire hovering over the playpen in the living room and kisses her, taking her whole ear into his mouth. Her singing voice skips and grates as she leans into him. She smiles. He can hear Maury Povich delivering his closing monologue on TV, which means that it's almost three o'clock, which means that he needs to get to school. He was caught stealing electronics components a few years ago and has to attend class every day as part of his probation. Most of his teachers don't seem to give a damn whether he shows up or not, but Mr. Taulbee, his English teacher, will have his ass in a sling if he's not there by three-fifteen. He'll be back in an hour or so, he tells Claire, and when he asks her if she wants him to pick up something to eat, she suggests Chinese food. Chinese it is, he says, as long as you promise to stop hiding my hairbands. He kisses her goodbye, and then pats Pierre the Second on the belly, and he drives to Springfield High School in their shaky old Plymouth.

Tommy Taulbee is already calling the last name on the roster, James Young, when his three missing students come through the door: Pierre Douglas, Chrissy Symancyk, and Ethan Hummer. They slump into their seats, sinking so far that he can barely see their faces, and he makes three quick checkmarks by their names. The way his students sit at their desks makes him think of miners being lowered into the earth, or moles disappearing into their burrows. His back winces just to look at them. It is the first time in more than a month that his entire class has been here, and he pauses to admire the descending row of identical checkmarks in his roster. He has always, ever since he was a boy, loved images like this: the clean downward repetition of signs and letters. He assigns his students a freewriting exercise on the topic of family, and for thirty minutes, while they scratch away with their pens and pencils, he grades the last of their papers from the day before. The wind pushing through the courtyard makes a sandy noise against the window. The PA system clicks once or twice and then falls silent. When their time is up, he collects his students' exercises from the front of the room and spends the last fifteen minutes of the hour giving them their next major assignment, which is due in mid-October. They have been studying African folklore in their textbook, and he wants them to write a folktale of their own, an original story that either teaches a lesson or presents the origin of something or relates the exploits of a god or a hero. After he has read the assignment to them, he says that he will be happy to answer any questions they have, and Melanie Sparks, who was Celia's baby-sitter, raises her hand and asks if her folktale can be a work of fiction.

Mr. Taulbee's mouth sneaks open in a sort of punctured smile before he seals it off. Yes, he says, the folktales they write can and in fact *should* be fiction. He does this sort of thing all the time, Melanie has noticed—answers her questions as though he were talking to the whole class. Whatever. She shuffles her deck of cards behind the broad shoulders of Danny Ergenbright, quietly folding them together, and lays out another hand of solitaire. When she uncovers the aces, she always fills them in this order: hearts for love, spades for skill, clubs for power, and diamonds for money. She feels like she is making a wish, and if she wins the game it will come true. Danny starts to slouch in his chair, exposing the top of her desk to Mr. Taulbee, and she takes her pen and raps him on that soft spot at the root of his skull. Sit up straight, she whispers, and he does, because he has a thing for her. For a few months after Celia disappeared, Melanie was afraid to leave her house. She imagined that she could be pulled out of her skin at any time, and she refused to go anywhere alone, not even to water the plants in her backyard. She would need every resource she had, she thought, all the power and skill in the world, just to walk safely out her own front door, and for a while she filled her aces in a different order: clubs, spades, hearts, and diamonds. She used to read Celia's favorite books to her, *Matilda* and *Lizard Music, Frindle* and *Charlotte's Web,* after they had finished their dinner and before she put her to bed. Melanie was fourteen back then, twice as old as Celia, and in a few years she will be twenty-one, one and a half times as old. When she thinks about her future, about graduating and going to college, getting married and having children, she imagines that she can feel Celia catching up to her, one and a third, one and a quarter, one and an eighth, breathing like a ghost across the soft hairs on the back of her neck. The bell rings on the other side of the courtyard, and the sixth- and seventh-graders come trickling and then pouring out of Springfield Middle School.

Melanie lays the five of hearts on top of the four, and the six on top of the five. Kristen Lanzetta can see her sitting at her desk, striped with sunlight from the windows at the back of the classroom, and these stripes, along with the bending limpness of her body, make her look like a stick of Juicy Fruit, Kristen's favorite chewing gum. The middle school lets out five minutes earlier than the high school. Kristen heads straight for the bus and takes her usual seat on the long bench at the back, beside her friend Andrea Onopa. When Kristen asks Andrea whether she's planning to go to the funeral tonight, Andrea says that she isn't sure, it depends on what her dad wants her to do. Well, I'm not going, Kristen says. Or at least she doesn't think she is. Celia was Kristen's best friend, but that was more than four years ago, an entire lifetime. She was only in the first grade then, and she is in the sixth now. The bus rumbles out of the parking lot, and she watches the telephone lines rise and fall outside the window. Her mother has explained to her how time thins out as you grow older, how the four years between seven and eleven are as long in their way—how they contain as much of your life—as the ten years between thirty and forty. Her mother says that life is like a pitcher filling with water, and unless you're one of those people who manages to forget her childhood as it passes, the pitcher will already be half-full by the time you're eighteen. It is an idea that has always frightened Kristen, and so she has tried hard to forget everything she possibly can: the names of her old teachers, the inside jokes she used to know, the movies she has seen. By now Celia is only a few whitened memories to her and a blurred feeling of sadness. The bus slows to take a speed bump, and, as always, as soon as the front wheels have thumped over, the bus driver accelerates, so that when the back wheels hit, the girls are bucked into the air, landing hard on their tailbones. When Kristen looks out the back window, she sees a thick band of clouds at the horizon, pressed together like rolls of fat. They are a charcoal black, though the rest of the sky is still open and blue. A police car glides in next to the bus at a stoplight, and the boy in front of her pumps his arm in the air as though the car were a tractor trailer, trying to get the police officer to sound his siren.

Kimson Perry gives the siren a single clipped *b-woop* and

then flashes his revolving lights, nodding at the boy on the bus, who is offering him the thumbs-up sign. When the stoplight changes he shoots along the reservoir toward home. It is nearly four-thirty, and he still has to shower and change for the memorial service. At the head of his block stands the Second Friendship Baptist Church, a small brick building with a cross on the roof that rotates in the wind like a weather vane, and as he turns the corner he brakes to read the signboard on the lawn:

NOTHING MAKES GOD LAUGH LIKE WHEN WE TELL
HIM OUR PLANS FOR THE FUTURE

As usual, he finds himself framing an argument against it. He is sure that what the sign means to suggest is that we don't need to worry, we're in good hands, but there is a certain thoughtless brutality to the message that disturbs him. After all, there are people in this world who know nothing but suffering. Their plans are all they have to live for. Which is to say that the message fails to give solace to the very people who might need it most. What kind of God would deny us so much, even the comfort of our wishes, he wonders. Kimson pulls into his driveway and unlocks his front door and then washes and shaves and tightens himself into his shirt and tie. More than 750,000 children are reported missing every year, but almost all of them are found within hours or days. Celia has been missing since March of 1997, and though he would never tell Janet this, he can't imagine that she isn't dead. What makes the case so goddamn frustrating is how little there is to go on, how little there ever was. There were no clues, no witnesses. She was playing in her own backyard. She had no reason to run away, and no one to run to. It has been more than a year since the tip-line has taken a phone call, and if it weren't for Janet, he is certain he would have allowed the case to go quietly inactive by now. He brushes his teeth, rinses the collar of foam from the bristles, and afterward drives to the pavilion, where the crowd for the memorial service is gathering. Janet is already there, standing beside her husband, and when Kimson hugs her hello, her lips graze his cheek and one of her knees knocks against him and he smells the peachlike fragrance of her shampoo. He is embarrassed to find himself becoming aroused.

Janet squeezes Kimson by the muscles of his upper arms and thanks him for coming, and when she lets him go, he takes her hand and says that of course he will always be there for her, she should know that, slipping his thumb ever so flickeringly into and out of her palm, like a minnow. She has been friends with Kimson for years now, sitting two chairs over from him in the community orchestra, where she plays clarinet and he plays contrabassoon, but ever since she lost her daughter she has spoken to him almost daily. He will even phone her in the evening occasionally—worried, he will say, that he hasn't heard from her during his shift. She has seen so many people this afternoon, though, accepted so many token condolences, that she doesn't have the energy to think about that thumb and what it might mean. She still loves her husband sometimes. She sinks her forehead onto her husband's shoulder for a moment, sighing, and then lifts her head and looks out over the guests. She sees Rollie and Judy and Andrea Onopa, Greg and Alma and Oscar Martin, Enid Embry, Sara Cadwallader, Tommy Taulbee and his father, Todd Paul. The wind has blown a shoal of rainclouds in from the east, so that half of the sky is a dense gray-black and the other half is filled with sunlight. The thick branches of an oak tree are rocking and creaking above the rows of folding chairs, and the skirt of Janet's newly purchased black dress keeps billowing taut between her legs. She sees Sheila and Tim Lanzetta, but not their daughter Kristen, holding a cane umbrella across their laps. She sees Melanie Sparks, Celia's old baby-sitter, who is standing at the margin of the grass, her arms wrapped around a lamppost she has pressed her ear to as though she were listening to vibrations from the ground. In the past four years Melanie might be the only person in town who has never told Janet what she should do to make herself feel better. She has been amazed at the number of people who seem to believe they know the answer, the one sure remedy she hasn't thought to try yet, everything from yoga to Prozac to deer hunting to a good hard cry. The Reverend Gautreaux, who is waiting on the steps of the pavilion, signals to Janet that she and Christopher can take their seats, and the two of them walk down the aisle to the front row.

The thing about cigarettes, the Reverend has discovered, is that when you breathe through them they breathe right back, like another set of lungs, and this sensation of having your breath returned to you, along with the almost respiratory heat of the smoke, makes smoking a cigarette very much like exchanging a kiss—but a kiss that you can control, measuring it out in increments, however shallow or deep you wish them to be. It is one of his pet theories that this, as much as the nicotine, is what makes it so hard to quit smoking. He waits for a few late arrivals to settle into their chairs and then stiffens his posture as a sign that everyone should fall quiet. He learned to do this— to broadcast this aura of preparedness, like a runner poised on his mark—within weeks of accepting his parish. It never fails to work. United States Congressman Asa Hutchinson, drinking from a paper bag in the corner of the pavilion, stops to blow his nose loudly, explosively, into a handkerchief. When the Reverend asked him earlier if he would mind moving into the chairs until the ceremony was over, the congressman's eyes flared into frightened blue stars and he gripped the banister behind his bench and said, You can't make me go, this is where I live. The Reverend can feel a crawling sort of itch in the back of his throat, but it is only five-thirty, and he has another two hours before he will be safely home to light another cigarette. He coughs and tells the congregation, those who are gathered here to remember Celia Brooks, that he will read to them first from the book of Jeremiah. When his father died, Reverend Gautreaux found that he had underlined more than a thousand verses in his Bible, some with a watery blue ink that had faded to the color of a robin's egg and others with a fluorescent yellow highlighter. This particular verse he had marked for some reason with a pair of stars and an exclamation point. The Reverend lifts the silk tail from his Bible, and Christopher listens as he begins to read.

For the hurt of the daughter of my people am I hurt; I am black; astonishment hath taken hold on me. Is there no balm in Gilead; is there no physician there? Why then is not the health of the daughter of my people recovered? The Reverend shuts his Bible and holds it against his stomach with both hands. Christopher watches the wind gather up his hair, tossing it about like streamers of grass, and listens as he says that it is hard for us not to react with anger, yes, with anger and confusion, when those we love are taken before their time. The air is piping through the trees, and his voice keeps rising and dropping away. Christopher is thinking about all the fathers he has read about, the ones who have lost their daughters to unknown circumstances, unknown powers, like the Arkansas millionaire who built a high stone wall around his house and then, when his daughter was returned to him, sank all his money into the world's largest display of Christmas lights, which he donated to Walt Disney World after his neighbors complained about the crowd of sightseers. The Reverend is talking about the difficulty of knowing the mind of God. Why does He allow so many of us to come to grief? Whose world are we living in, after all? Christopher can feel his eyes stinging in the wind, but the eyedrops he bought are still at home in the medicine cabinet. It is only a few minutes later, when the Reverend says his daughter's name again, Celia Elizabeth Brooks, and then something about how as long as we remember her she is inside all of us, that United States Congressman Asa Hutchinson begins to shout.

The congressman slashes his arms through the air in a wild X, the bottle in his hand whipping this way and that so that arcs of brass-colored liquor keep spattering onto the floor of the pavilion. She's already dead, he cries, you can't do this again, my wife is already dead. He can hear the distant chop of the reservoir, see the people in their folding chairs paused in a faraway stillness, but everything around him seems to be wrapped in a layer of wool. All his attention is gathered around the man in the black robe, a bat, who has been mocking his Elizabeth. He thinks of her burial plot, so many miles away, already scattered with the first few leaves of autumn. In October, when he travels north, he sees entire flocks of swallows and robins migrating south for the winter, thousands of them flying in clots and waves, and he imagines that he is a counterweight connected to them by an invisible steel rod, balancing their motion with his own. For a while, during the final months of his wife's illness, the wasting smell of her body made him sick to his stomach, and he had to wear a surgical mask over his face as he washed and fed her. He has never forgiven himself. He watches the Reverend Gautreaux walking slowly toward him, palms extended, asking him to calm down, calm down, saying that everything will be all right. How dare he! The congressman hurls his liquor bottle at the man, but it rolls past his shoulder and hits one of the columns, shattering inside its paper bag with a heavy concussive sound. Sara Cadwallader and Sheila and Tim Lanzetta, who are sitting across the aisle from Celia's parents in the front row, leap at the noise and skip back from their chairs.

Sara Cadwallader watches the Reverend back carefully away from the crazy man in gray clothing, moving with such an awkwardly wooden gait that he reminds her of her cats, Mudpie and Thisbe, treading over the floor vent in her living room, shaking their feet after each step as though their pads were sticking to the metal. The Reverend moves slowly down the stairs, stopping finally in the aisle beside her, and the crazy man looks away from him for a moment, right into Sara's eyes. He has a crusted shaving cut above his lip, and his corneas are stained a pale yellow, and she has a curious desire to wave to him. Then he seems to notice the rest of the people in the crowd. He says something she does not understand and climbs onto his bench and from there into the rafters of the pavilion, shouting, Stay away from me, keep away, and glass liquor bottles begin raining down from him in twos and threes, breaking against the railing or bouncing and sailing into the chairs. There are so many of them that she thinks he must have hundreds up there. She takes cover behind the Reverend, who himself takes cover behind a wastebasket. Sara lives two houses down from the Brookses, and when Celia was seven years old, she used to invite her over for Kool-Aid and cookies and let her play with Mudpie and Thisbe. They were just kittens then, and they would press against Celia and purr, slinking through her ankles and collapsing onto her feet. It is hard for Sara to believe that someone so young could come and go from the world so quickly. Maybe she is not really gone, though, Sara thinks. Maybe no one is ever really gone. Maybe when we die we simply drift in and out of the people we have left behind, touching each of them in turn, like God does. This is what she likes to imagine, at least. She watches a few of the bigger men go in after the crazy person, braving the shower of glass inside the pavilion, but it is Rollie Onopa who manages to hoist himself into the rafters.

Rollie crawls over the dusty wooden beams on his hands and the balls of his feet, keeping to the outside edge of the pavilion, where the ceiling slants down to the narrowest wedge of space. Leaves and candy wrappers and potato chip bags have collected there in a deep hummock, and though they crumple beneath him with a sound like burning kindling, the congressman is too busy taking aim at all the people below to notice him. Rollie sees three long rows of bottles behind the congressman, green and brown and crystal-clear—several years' worth of determined drinking, he would guess. He creeps along one of the cross-beams, approaching his quarry from behind. There is a flat, circular bird's nest the size of a Frisbee in his path, and when he crawls over it he sees that it was actually constructed *inside* a Frisbee. He has a keen admiration for birds, for their grace and beauty and cleverness, but bird lovers have always seemed a bit nutty to him, and he doesn't like to tell people about it. Stealing up on the congressman, he feels like he did as a child playing spy, when the giddy hammering of his heart never quite made him laugh but always came close. Before the congressman can turn around, Rollie grabs him in a bear hug. In the moment of silence that follows, he hears his daughter saying that her dad will catch him, you just watch, he's probably got him already. When he tucks her in at night and she asks him if he loves her, he always says, Honey, you're the whole ball of wax, and she answers, Dad, that's really gross. The congressman tosses his head back and forth, growling, That's-e-nough, one slow syllable at a time. He bucks against Rollie, and Rollie loses hold of him. Then, before he can stop him, the congressman tumbles backward out of the rafters, knocking his head on the ceiling, and falls lurching and thrashing into the arms of the men below.

Rollie leaps to the floor and helps them carry him down the stairs, past the chairs and the lamps and the picnic tables, and past Enid Embry, who is already tidying up the shards of broken glass, sweeping them into a single long drift with the edge of her foot. This afternoon a guest on *The Art Bell Show* said that aliens have infiltrated every town in America, disguising themselves as drifters, and Enid would not be at all surprised if United States Congressman Asa Hutchinson were one of them. Nothing is beyond explanation. Just look at all the trouble he has caused, not to mention the mess he has made. He is lucky that nobody got killed. She listens to him yelling, Don't hit me, let me go, thy rod and thy staff, thy rod and thy staff, as those brave men pin his arms and legs to the ground and try to calm him down. After she has finished sweeping the glass from the first row of chairs, she brushes every last speck of it onto a sheet of cardboard that she finds lying by the wastebasket and throws it all away. There, she thinks. She has done her part. Everyone who hasn't wandered over to help subdue the congressman is standing before the pavilion, watching and whispering, except for the Reverend, who is sitting with his head on his knees, and Janet, who is busy smoothing a line of ointment over a cut on Kimson Perry's hand. The stormclouds have unfolded across most of the sky, and when Enid gazes out at the reservoir, she can see a thin blade of sunlight receding over the water. There is no rain, but listening closely she can hear a faint grumble of thunder, and she looks overhead, waiting for the first spark of lightning to flash. She sees a movement in the sky, swift and erratic, a sudden darting flicker of UFO gray, and feels a fish-hook catch of excitement in her chest. But it is only a squirrel, high in the branches of an oak tree, swaying back and forth in the wind.

The Green Children

—based on an account in the *Historia rerum Anglicarum,* written in
1196 by William of Newburgh—

They say I was the first to touch them. When the reapers found the children in the wolf-pits—a boy and a girl, their skin the pale flat green of wilting grass—they shuddered and would not lay hands on them, prodding them across the fields with the handles of their scythes. I watched them approach from my stone on the bank of the river. The long, curving blades of the scythes sent up flashes of light that dazzled my eyes and made me doubt what I was seeing—a boy and a girl holding fast to each other's garments, twisting them nervously between their green fingers, their green faces turned to the sun. The reapers nudged and jabbed at them until they came to a stop at my side, where the river's green water lapped at their shoes. I allowed myself to stare.

Alden took me by the shoulder and said, "We think that it must be the rotting disease. They were calling out when we found them, but none of us could make out the tongue. We're taking them to the house of Richard de Calne."

I understand little of medicine, and in those days I understood even less, but I could see that, despite the coloring of their skin, the children were healthy. The veins beneath their arms were dark and prominent, the sharp green of clover or spinach leaves. Their breathing was regular and clear.

"Will you carry them across the river?" Alden asked me, and I took my time before answering, cleaning the gristle from my teeth with the tapering edge of a twig. I know the rules of bargaining.

"Two coins," I said. "Two coins for each. And one for the rest of you."

The reapers fished the silver from their satchels.

If I was not the first to touch the children, I was certainly the first to carry them.

I lifted the boy onto my shoulders (one of the men had to rap the girl's wrist with the butt of his scythe to make her let go of him) and was halfway across the river when Alden summoned me back. "Take some of us across first. If you leave the boy there alone, he'll run away." So I carried two of the men to the opposite shore, and then the boy, and then I returned for the girl, balancing her in the crook of my arm so that she straddled the hummock of muscle like a rider on a pony. This was years ago, when I could haul a full trough of water all the way from the river to the stables, or raise a calf over my head, or shore up the wall of a house while the sun dried the foundation. The water was as high as my waist when my foot fell on a patch of thick, jelly-like moss and shot into the current. The girl wrapped her arms around my neck and began to speak in a panic, a thread of shrill, gabbling syllables that I could not understand. "Wooramywoorismifath!"

I regained my balance, throwing my arms out, and heard one of the reapers laughing at me from the riverbank. The girl was crying now, convulsive sobs that shook her entire body, and I took her chin in my fingers and turned her face toward mine. Her eyes were as brown as singed barley, as brown as my own. "I know these people," I said to her. "Look at me. I know them. No one will hurt you." A yellow slug of mucus was trailing from her nose, and I wiped it off with my finger and slung it into the water, where the fish began to nip at it. "Don't cry," I said, and with three loping strides I set her on the other shore.

As the reapers led the children into Woolpit, I kneaded the coins in my pocket, feeling their satisfying weight and the imprint of their notches. Seven birds came together in the sky. The coming week would bring a change of fortune. It was the plainest of signs.

The river spills straight through the center of town, with the fields, the church, and the stables on one side and the smithy, the tavern, and the market on the other. It is an angry foaming dragon, the current swift and violent, and only the strongest can cross it without falling. The nearest stepway is half an hour's walk downstream, a wedge of stone so slippery it seems to sway beneath you like a lily pad, yet before I took my place on the shore, the people of Woolpit made that journey every day. I was just a boy then and liked to stand on the bank casting almond shells into the water, following beside them as they tumbled and sailed away, memorizing the trails they took. By the time my growth came upon me I knew the river well, every twist and eddy and surge of it. I soon discovered I could cross it with ease. I had found my work.

The days after the green children appeared were busy ones. I would rest on my stone no longer than a moment before a new party of townspeople would arrive, their coins gleaming in their hands, eager to see the wonders at the house of Richard de Calne. One by one I would hoist them onto my back and wade into the water, leaning against the current and rooting my feet to the ground, and one by one I would haul them back to the other shore when they returned some few hours later. At night, as I lay on my pallet, the muscles of my back gave involuntary jerking pulses, like fish pulled from the river and clapped onto a hard surface. The sensation was entirely new to me then, though I have experienced it many times since.

The people who had seen the green children spoke of little else, and I listened to their accounts as they gathered in clutches on the strand:

"The girl is covered in bug bites, and the boy just lies there and shivers."

"I hear that de Calne has hired someone to train them in English."

"Green to their gums! Green to the roots of their hair!"

"Have you seen the midget who lives at Coggeshall Abbey?"

"I made a farting noise with my tongue, and the girl smiled at me."

"The chirurgeon says that it's chlorosis—the greensickness."

"They're the ugliest specimens I've ever seen—uglier than a boil, uglier than that hag Ruberta."

"I can see them glowing like marshfire when I close my eyes."

"Did I tell you my milk cow dropped a two-headed calf last year?"

"Mark my words—they'll be dead before the first frost."

The river was swollen with rain from a storm that had broken in the hills, but the sky over Woolpit was so windless and fine that the current ran almost noiselessly between its banks. As I carried the townsfolk through water as high as my gut, I gave my ear to them and learned that the green children had eaten nothing for several days, though bread and meat and greens had all been set before them. I learned that though they did not eat, they did drink from the dippers of water they were given, and that sometimes the girl even used the excess to clean her face and hands. One of the men who had examined the children for hidden weapons said that their hair was handsomely clipped, their teeth straight and white, and their clothing was stitched from a strange-looking material with many narrow furrows: it fell on their bodies with the stiffness of leather, yet was soft and smooth to the touch. "They huddled together as soon as I drew away," I heard him say. "They clutched their stomachs and cried."

On the third day of the children's keeping, one of the growers brought them some beans newly cut from the field. The children were plainly excited and slit the stalks open with their fingernails, examining the hollows for food, but finding nothing there, they began to weep. Then one of the kitchen maids swept the stalks aside and showed them how to crack open the pods. She prised out a row of naked beans, and the children gasped and thrust their hands out for them. The kitchen maid insisted on softening the beans in water first, and then, with great relish, the children devoured them. For several days after they would eat nothing else.

It was Martin, the tanner's son, who told me that the girl had spoken her name. He arrived at the river one evening carrying a palm-shaped basket of green reeds raddled so carelessly together that the fringe twisted in every direction. "Our fire went out," he said. "My dad told me to go get some more."

"Climb on," I said, and he shinnied up to my shoulders. As we crossed the water, he asked me whether I had seen the boy and the girl yet.

"I have," I told him.

"Did you know the girl's started talking now? Real words, I mean."

"What has she said?"

"She can say 'water,' and she can say 'hungry,' and she can say 'more.' The boy hasn't said a damned thing, though." We had reached the shore by then, and I lifted him from my shoulders, straight into the air, so that he spat the word "Jesus" and then laughed as I planted him upright on the bank. "That's what my dad told me, anyway," and he ran up the trail into the village.

When he returned some short time later, there was a small heap of orange coals smoldering inside his basket. Each time the breeze touched them, they glimmered brightly for a moment, then gently dimmed. "You're not going to spill those on me, are you?" I asked. "Because if you do you'll be walking home wet."

"I promise," he said, and so I carried him to the other shore.

As I stood him on dry ground I asked, "Has the girl told her name yet?"

"Seel-ya," he said. "That's how she pronounced it, too. Funny." He set his basket of coals on the grass and pulled a coin from the inside of his shoe: it was clinging to the skin of his foot, and he had to peel it loose before handing it to me. I took the coin and dropped it in my satchel, heavy as a fist from the day's business.

"Goodbye, then," he said.

"Goodbye," I answered.

He marched off toward home, carrying his pocket of light into the graying air.

It was no later than the hunter's moon when the first travelers began to arrive. They came from the east and the south (those from the west and north having no need to cross the river) and asked how to find their way to the green children they had heard tell of. They referred to the children as oddities, or marvels, or curiosities. Some of them had been given to believe they were bedded down like goats or cattle in a grain-crib or a stable somewhere, though in truth de Calne was housing them in one of his servants' rooms. "You'll find them over there," I told them, gesturing obscurely beyond a spinney of thin, girlish elm trees. "A large house past a row of small ones. You can't miss it." I offered to ferry them to the opposite shore of the river on my back. "Only two coins," I would say—my new fee for pilgrims. "Or you can try to push your way across without me." At this I would toss a stick into the water, dropping it midstream so that the current gripped it immediately, wrenching it away. "There's an outcropping of rocks downstream where we usually retrieve the bodies."

The travelers all carried parcels and walking sticks, and after scouting along the bank for a time they always accepted my offer.

The green children had quickly become commonplace to the people of Woolpit, just another feature of the landscape, like the bluff above the maple thicket, shaped like the body of a sleeping horse, or the trio of stone wells outside the marketplace, but as the story of their discovery spread, the people who came to see them journeyed from farther and farther away. I was becoming a wealthy man.

One of these pilgrims, a boy of no more than fifteen who was traveling alone, asked me why there was no bridge by which to make the crossing. "We've built them before," I said, "but the river is too powerful. They never last the month before the rains come and the high water washes them away."

"There's a man in my town who's developed a new method of working with stone. He can shape it into a half-circle, and it will be broad enough and strong enough for even a man on horseback to pass over. I've seen him do it. For the right price, I'm sure he would build a bridge for you."

I gave the boy a flinty stare and said, "We have no need of such a service." His hair was as white as an old man's, with the flat shine of chalk. Even after he was gone, its image stayed in my eyes.

As soon as the green children began to eat the same food as the rest of us, the same bread and flesh and vegetables, the girl developed a healthy cushion of skin around her bones. The boy, however, became frailer and more feverish with each new morning, trembling with the slightest movement of the air and passing a pungent, oily shit from his bowels. A doctor bled and purged him to balance his humours, then applied a poultice to his sores, but to no effect. He merely rolled over onto his side, coughing and blinking until he fell asleep. For a single coin Richard de Calne would have his clothes stripped from him so that onlookers could see the way his skin pinched tight around the corners of his body—a mottled shade of green, like a leaf fed upon by aphids.

The boy had yet to say anything more than his name, a dusty line of syllables I have long since forgotten, but the girl, Seel-ya, was now speaking in complete sentences, and she astonished her visitors by conversing with them in a tongue they under-stood, telling the tale of how she came to this country.

She was, she said, from a wholly different land, though she could not say where it lay in relation to our own. The people there were of her color, and when she first saw the reapers lean-ing over her in the wolf-pits, their skin was of so pale a shade she was not sure they were human, and she screamed for her mother and father. The sun, she claimed, was not so bright in her country, and the stars were not so many. She had been play-ing outside her house when she heard a great sound, like the chiming of bells, and when she turned to follow it, she found herself in this place. The boy had appeared in the wolf-pits alongside her, and though she did not know him, she could tell that he came from her land. She missed her family, she said, and she wanted to go home.

One morning, while I was waiting for my first foot passen-gers of the day, Joana the Cyprian came walking toward the river. It has been a long time now since she was young enough to sell her services, but in the years of which I speak she was the most beautiful woman in Woolpit, and her eyes in their black rings were as shining and open as windows. She lived in a small hut hidden in the trees at the edge of town. The sun was climb-ing into the sky behind her, and through the thin fabric of her dress I could see the outline of her thighs and a tangled gusset of pubic hair. "Good morning, Curran," she said to me.

"Joana." I nodded.

"Aren't you going to ask me what I'm doing out so early?" Instead I pitched a stone into the water to measure the pace of the current, watching as it drifted from the surface to the bed. "I'm headed to Richard de Calne's house," she said.

"Going to gawp at the green children, I suspect."

"Going to *work* with the green children." Her voice was thistleish with irritation, and I had to smother a grin. It was one of my joys to provoke her. "I'm teaching the girl her duties as a woman," she said. "De Calne plans to raise her to his wife." She swung the copper-colored horsetail of her hair over her shoulder. "So are you going to take me across or not?"

I slapped my palms against my back and said, "I'm at your service, dear," but she winked at me and declared, "No, Curran, I want to ride up front"—which is exactly what she did. She wrapped her legs around my hips and her arms around my neck. I swung forward with her into the river.

As I carried her deeper into the water, she allowed herself to sink slowly down over my crotch, exaggerating her fall with each jerk of my stride. The muscles of the current pulled at my ankles. I could feel her releasing her breath in a long, thin rope against my chest, and my nose began to prickle with her scent. "Why so quiet, Curran?" she asked. "Hmm?" When I set her on the other shore, she placed a slow-rolling kiss on my lips and ran her finger up my penis, from the root to the ember, which was visibly propping up my waistcloth. "So what do I owe you?" she whispered into my ear.

I brought her hand to my mouth and kissed the knuckles. "No charge," I said.

Sometimes I wish it was still that way.

I was leaning forward on my stone, eating a boiled egg one of the farmers had given me for his passage, on the morning the monk arrived. I watched him hobble around the end of the stables and follow the path toward the river. His robe was coated so thickly with dust I could not tell whether the cloth underneath was brown or white. "Tell me," he asked, planting his staff at my feet, "have I reached Woolpit?"

"You have." I cast the eggshell halves into the water, where they went bobbing off like two glowing boats. I have watched the river for many years, and there is nothing it won't carry away. I'm told that if you follow it far enough into the distance, past the hills and the long forest of pines, it empties into the sea, offering its cargo of sticks, bones, and eggshells to the whales, but I have never been that far.

"I've come for the monsters," said the monk. The sun shifted from behind a cloud, and he squinted into the glare.

"The children, you mean." I pointed across the river. "They're at the house of Richard de Calne."

"The soldier," he said. "Yes, so I've heard. How much for passage?"

"Three coins," I said. He drew open the pouch that was sagging from his belt, handed me the silver, and then rapped my leg with the end of his staff. "Up," he ordered.

I looked at him grayly. He was not a large man and I could have broken him over my knee, but instead I pocketed the coins, counting repeatedly to three in my head.

While we were crossing the river, I allowed him to slip a few notches lower on my spine so that the hem of his robe trailed in the water and took on weight. Snake-shapes of dirt twisted away from him downstream, but he did not notice. He told me that he had heard of the green children from a beggar in the town of Lenna, who had informed him fully of their strange condition. "They speak a language known to no Christian ear," the monk recited, "and are green as clover. The girl is loose and wanton in her conduct, and the boy shudders at the touch of any human hand. They are a corruption to all those who look upon them."

"Most of what you say is false," I said. A little whirlpool spun like a plate on the surface of the water before it wobbled and came apart. "The children have learned our own tongue now, or at least the girl has, and while I can't speak for anyone else, they've certainly done me no harm."

"You've seen them?" he asked.

"I have, and they're no danger to anyone."

He made a scoffing noise. "Yes, but you are clearly an ignorant man. I'm told they will eat nothing but beans. Beans! Beans are the food of the dead, and the dead-on-earth are the implements of Satan."

"They eat flesh and bread, just like the rest of us. It was only those first few days that they ate beans."

"The devil quickly learns to hide himself," he said dismissively, as though he had tired of arguing with me. "I aim to baptize them, and if they won't take the water, then I aim to kill them."

I stopped short, anchoring my foot against the side of a rock. I could feel the anger mounting inside me. "You won't harm them," I said.

"I will do as my conscience demands." He cuffed my ear. "Now move, you!"

At that, I whipped my body around and let him drop into the water. He sideslipped downstream, tumbling and sputtering in a fog of brown soot, before he managed to find root on the riverbottom. Then, bracing himself with his staff, which swayed and buckled in his hands, he hitched his way slowly to the other shore. By the time he staggered onto the rocks, I was already sitting against the high ledge of the bank. His robe hung on his body like a moulting skin, and his hair curtained his eyes. "You—!" he said. He flapped his arms and water spattered onto the shingle. "I want my silver returned to me."

I did not feel the need to answer him. Instead, I reached into my pocket and retrieved the coins, slinging them at him one by one. They thumped against the front of his robe and fell to the rocks with a ting. He picked them up, then straightened himself and set his eyes on me. "I have a mission," he said. "God has given it to me. I will not be discouraged from it by the muscles of any Goliath," and he went stamping up the road into Woolpit, wringing the water from his clothing. Three blackbirds landed in the path behind him, striking at the dirt.

It was late that afternoon when I heard that the boy had died.

I abandoned my post by the river that night to attend the burning of his body. The pyre had been laid with branches of white spruce and maple, and the silver wood of the one and the gold wood of the other carried a gentle, lambent glow that seemed to float free of the pyre in the air. The moon was full, and I could see the faces of the townspeople by its light. Alden was there, and Joana, and the boy Martin, along with the blacksmith and the reapers and all the other men and women of Woolpit. I had never seen so many of them gathered together in one place. The monk, though, was nowhere among them. He had indeed baptized the children, I learned—immersing them in a basin of water, each for the count of one hundred—but while the girl had survived the dunking, the boy had not. He was already weak with illness, and when his body met the water, it stiffened in a violent grip and went still as the monk pushed him under. One of the servants who was watching said that he breathed not a single bubble of air. When de Calne learned that the boy had died, he set his men on the monk with clubs, and the monk was made to flee by the western road.

There was some discussion between de Calne and Father Gervase, the town priest, as to whether or not the boy ought to be buried in church ground—had his spirit passed from him before, during, or after baptism?—but finally it was decided to follow the path of caution. They would allow the fire to consume him.

The boy was laid out on the pyre inside a white sheet painted with wax, and as we stood about the fallow field watching, de Calne signaled to his servants and a ring of torches was driven into the wood. The flames were tall and bright, the smoke so thickly woven that it blotted out the stars. Our faces were sharp in the yellow light, which was clear and steady, so that our shadows scarcely wavered. I saw the green girl holding on to Joana, her arms wrapped tightly around her waist. A moment later de Calne stooped at her side, taking her chin in his hands. He stared into her eyes with a strange, questioning zeal until she quailed away from him, hiding her face in Joana's dress.

The fire burned long into the night, and I fell into conversation with the merchant brothers Radulphi and Emmet. They were deliberating over what had killed the boy, and they had flatly differing notions on the matter, as they had on so many others. "He was not of this world," said Emmet. "That much was clear to see—and so, of course, he rejected the baptism. The sacraments are for members of the body of Jesus Christ. The boy was a member of no body but his own."

"But the girl accepted the water without sign of affliction." Radulphi smacked his palms together as he made his point. "And it's not at all clear that the children are from another world. They might have gotten lost in the flint mines of Fordham, nothing else, and simply wandered around the mine shafts until they came out inside the wolf-pits. It's happened before."

"Then how do you explain the color of their skin?" I asked.

"It was the greensickness, like the chirurgeon said."

"Not likely," said Emmet. "And if it wasn't the baptism that killed the boy, then what was it?"

"Starvation," said Radulphi. "His body wasn't accepting the food he ate, and so it devoured itself."

"At the very moment he touched the water?" Emmet smacked his own palms together. "Hah!"

Radulphi had been working an acorn between his fingers, and he tossed it to me. "You haven't told us what you think, Curran."

"What do I think?" I was, as I have said, a young man then, and my answer was a young man's answer: "I think it's foolish to argue over matters that cannot be decided. Who knows why our spirits depart, and who can say where they go when they do? These things are a mystery. Nothing more can be said."

I have grown older since then, if only occasionally wiser, but I have tried to pay attention to what happens around me, and there is one sure thing my age has taught me: death is no mystery, in its cause if not in its consequences. If Radulphi were to ask me his question today, my answer would not be the same.

I would tell him instead what I have seen with my own eyes: you can die of too much, and you can die of too little, and everybody dies of one or the other. That night, however, I simply fell silent. The shadow of the boy's body flickered in and out of sight inside the flames, and as the wood settled, de Calne's men prodded at it with long, forked sticks to keep it from tumbling free.

"I still believe it was the baptism," said Emmet.

"And I still believe you're an idiot," said Radulphi.

I cast the acorn into the fire, listening for the nut to explode in the heat.

It was ten years or more before I saw the girl again. The last of the trees were turning color with the end of autumn, and the air had the fine, dry smell of burning leaves that signals an early snow. I was resting against the edge of my stone, worn smooth from all my years of sitting, when a young woman emerged from the spinney of elm trees by the tavern. She walked swiftly but deliberately, turning occasionally to look behind her as though sweeping the ground for footprints. I crossed the river to be ready to meet her on the other bank.

"I need passage over the water," she said when she arrived. Her breath was coming rapidly, in thick white plumes. "Quickly. How much?" she asked.

"Four coins," I said.

She counted out the money from a leather satchel hanging at her side. A shirt that had been tucked neatly inside poked out from the broaching after she tied the straps down. "Is there anybody following me?" she asked.

The sky was hidden behind a single flat sheet of clouds, and the path into town was long and shadowless. Even the birds were resting.

"No one," I said.

"Good." She handed me the silver, then shifted her satchel so that it fell over her buttocks and climbed onto my back. "Let's go."

The water was frigid that morning. It rose around my stomach in a sealed, constricting ring, and I began to shiver. I couldn't help myself. Even the year before, the chill of the water had seemed only the barest prickle to me, a tiny gnat to swat away with my fingers, but with each passing month, ever since the summer had fallen, I had noticed it more and more. The young woman tightened her arms around my chest and said, "I hate this—crossing the water. I feel sick inside."

"Don't worry," I said. "I won't let anything happen to you."

It was then that she made a clicking noise in her throat, and I could feel her seizing upon a memory or perception. You learn to recognize such things when you carry people as I do: it's in their posture and their breathing and the power of their grip. In this case, it was as if all the heaviness drained from her body into mine, then gradually returned to her. "I remember you," she said. "You were here by the river on the day I came."

Whereupon I realized who she was.

Her body had spread open into its grown-up shape and become paler over time. Her skin was now a yellow-gold, like that of the spice merchants who travel through Woolpit from Far Asia.

"Seel-ya," I said.

"That's right."

"You look—different."

She almost smiled. "I know. I lost most of my color a long time ago. The chirurgeon says it was the change in my diet, but people take on new colors all the time as they grow older, don't they? They're like caterpillars turning into butterflies." She tensed suddenly. "Tell me, is there anybody following me yet?"

I looked behind me. "Still no one."

"Good," she said, and her muscles relaxed. "Then so far he hasn't realized."

I bent my thoughts to what she had said about people taking on new colors. It was not without its truth. The tillers and planters, for instance, were gray with a soil that would never wash out of their skin—you could recognize them by the stain of it on their hands and faces—and my own body had turned a rich chestnut-brown across the chest and shoulders from the hours I spent in the sun. Children were born with murky blue eyes, and only later did they become green or brown or hazel, or the lighter, more natural blue of the living. Old people faced with their last sickness turned white as tallow as they took to their beds. I caught my likeness in the water and saw the two long cords of silver in my hair. I deposited Seel-ya on the shore.

"Where are you fleeing to, child?" I asked.

"How do you know that I'm fleeing?"

I gave a snort of laughter, and her face sprang up in a slanting grin. "Very well," she said. "I suppose I have to tell somebody. I'm going to King's Lynne. There's a man that I intend to wed." She glanced over my shoulder, across the river. "In fact"—she dug into her satchel for another four coins—"if Richard de Calne or any of his servants come asking after me, will you tell them you haven't seen me? Or better yet, will you send them the wrong way?"

"I will," I told her, and I pocketed the coins. "Good luck to you."

She nodded. She lifted herself carefully onto the shelf of the bank, then turned back to me.

"You were kind to me that day. I haven't forgotten. Thank you."

"You were in need of someone's kindness," I said.

She set out along the southern road, moving at a steady trot, and soon she vanished from my sight behind the stables. That was the last I saw of her.

What else is there to tell? De Calne and his men did indeed come looking for the girl, their pikestaffs held at the ready, and I directed them into the hills to the west of town, where a few meager paths had been trampled into the brush by the few travelers foolish enough to attempt passage. Packs of wolves and wild boar could be heard baying and grunting there at night, and great owls lifted from the branches of trees with a sound like someone beating the dirt from a mat.

I told de Calne that the girl said she was going to gather her strength there and make her way north when the weather cleared. He and his men came stumping back two days later, their garments split and tattered and their pikestaffs left behind them in the forest.

The winter that followed was the coldest I have ever seen. (It has been a long life, and I cannot imagine I will see one colder.) The river froze over for the first time in memory, assuming the blue-white color of solid ice, and the people of Woolpit scattered dirt across it in a continuous sheet, walking from one shore to the other as though it were simply a road. I spent the season hauling coal to the village from the mines. When spring came and the water melted, the chalk-haired boy who had visited Woolpit ten years before—I had never forgotten him—returned with the stonemason he had told me of. Together they built a bridge that spanned the water in a perfect arch. It stands there still, as sturdy and elegant as the bones of a foot.

I found new work as a lifter and plougher, and when my strength went, as a tavern-keeper. It was some few years ago that a man of Newburgh, a historian by the name of William, came to the tavern seeking reports of the green children, and I told him this story as I have told it to you. Afterward, he asked me if I knew what had become of the girl. Had she married the man at King's Lynne? Had de Calne ever managed to find her? Though I am certain she did not return to Woolpit, and de Calne soon gave her up as lost, I know nothing else for a certainty. Some say she did indeed marry, mothering children of her own. Some say she took work as a kitchen steward in a small town to the south of Norfolk. Some say she vanished from this world as suddenly as she appeared here, following a sound like the chiming of bells. I myself could make no guesses. It was very long ago, and I was not there.

As the Deck Tilted
into the Ocean

It is no miracle, she says.
A husband drives away,
the world clicks shut
like a little dead door.
If I could go to a movie
that lasted longer than my life
it might be alright.

—NAOMI SHIHAB NYE

There was *Ponette*, for instance, with sweet-faced Victoire Thivi-sol, four years old and artlessly sad, clinging to her rag doll Yoyotte. Janet watched the movie with an attention so perfect that it later surprised her, sinking into her chair until she was nothing but a pair of eyes and a bare reacting heart. She sat absolutely motionless, breathing slowly, as Ponette placed her doll on her mother's coffin, and as her cousins Matthias and Delphine convinced her to hide inside a Dumpster, where the lid fell shut around her fingers, and as her father went booming after her across the field by her aunt's house, sparklike insects dipping and spinning through the tall grass behind him. Janet heard herself making distant noises as she watched, chirps and gasps and ohs, the kind of sounds a bird might make. She couldn't help herself. It was the first movie she saw after the incident with her daughter, though afterward there were many others.

There was *The Sweet Hereafter*—starring Ian Holm, the android from *Alien*, and Sarah Polley, the small girl from *The Adventures of Baron Munchausen*—with its school bus gliding serenely off the edge of the road and resting for a long moment above the frozen lake, as still as a glass on a table. Janet almost believed the children inside would be okay, though she had already seen their grieving parents, and when the ice collapsed and the bus dropped through the rift, she felt an actual physical twist inside her, a feeling that did not soften until long after the movie's final image—a rotating Ferris wheel, body after body whirling off the edge of the screen.

There was *Mother,* playing at the Springfield Bargain Eight, with Albert Brooks and Debbie Reynolds and that wonderfully thorny scene where she feeds him the frost-staled sherbet from her freezer and his entire face cocks to one side. When he complained that the sherbet tasted "like an orange foot," Janet laughed, her voice ringing out in the quarter-light of the theater, and a shock of guilt passed through her. It was the first time she could remember laughing since her daughter had vanished. Her life had become a series of such firsts—the first time she had sex again, did the laundry again, read a book again. The first time she sang along with the radio or went to church again.

There was even *Titanic,* which despite its dialogue—as clumsy as any she had ever heard, like a top-heavy drunk swaying into the walls—she found quite moving. She witnessed the movie from a wide space of sorrow inside her that she had only recently discovered, and the thousand images of the ship as it foundered seemed to reach into that space and cut at her. The water streaming under the bed of the elderly couple. The preacher declaiming madly from his Bible. The night after she saw it she actually dreamed she was on board, watching from the rail as the deck tilted into the ocean.

She usually went to matinee showings, sometimes three or four or five a week, when the lobbies were deserted and the ushers stood around the snack bar eating handfuls of popcorn from the popcorn bin. The video games, when she stepped too close to them, called out to her like carnival barkers, their booming voices abraded with static. LOOK ALIVE, SOLDIER! they said, or WHO DARES TO DISTURB THE DRAGON'S LAIR? and she always took care to walk on the opposite side of the foyer. It was not so much that she was startled by them—though she was, a little: lately she winced at even the slightest disturbance, like a newborn baby who could not yet distinguish between noise and the threat of pain—but because she treasured whatever small anonymity she could find and did not like to draw attention to herself. No matter how often she went to the movies, no one there seemed to remember her, and it was a relief. Everywhere else she went she was Janet, the woman whose daughter had disappeared, slipped away from her outside her very own home, poor Janet, the mother of that girl who went missing, you know the one, Celia.

There was *Kolya, Boogie Nights,* and *Shall We Dance?* There was *One True Thing* and *A Bug's Life.*

She liked it best when the theater was empty. She would slip through the doors and find a seat on the aisle, two-thirds of the way from the front, where she could sink down into herself and listen to the music, waiting for the lights to dim. In the smallest screening room of the Reservoir Ten she had discovered a chair with a busted mounting fixture, and she tried to sit directly behind it whenever she could, since anyone who leaned their weight into it would list backward until they lay staring at the ceiling from her lap, then apologize and move to the next row. It was important to her that her view be unobstructed. She was rarely alone in the theater (though for *Ponette* she was, and for *The Boxer,* and, years before, when she was a college student, for *Dreamchild*), and even during the early minutes of the film, after the trailers had finished, other people would often wander in and search for a seat, sending a sharp wedge of light down the aisle that would gradually close like a fan. They came by themselves or with their children—there were almost never any couples at weekday matinees. The bigger children, four or five years old, liked to gather in strings along the first few rows. They sipped Icees through long straws and tossed hard pips of popcorn at each other. They dropped pennies and rubber balls into the aisle. They ran to the bathroom clutching their genitals when they had to pee. The younger children liked to sit on their mothers' laps—tugging at their clothing, turning their faces to their chests whenever they became frightened. Janet felt the pull of her own motherhood as she watched them, that simple intuitive hunger for the touch of a child. She only went to G-rated movies when she wanted to punish herself.

As the last few degrees of light thinned away, a deep, breathing silence would fill the theater, broken only by the faint rattle of the projector, and the production symbol would appear on screen, a spinning globe, perhaps, or a boy fishing from the moon, and then the movie would begin. At that moment part of Janet—that part of her which believed in stories as though they were more real than her own life—always seemed to filter from her skin into the surrounding air. If the movie was a good one, she would lose sight of everything else until the final credits rolled. She would forget about the other people in the theater, the burning of the safety lights, the opening and closing of the rear door. She would no longer be able tell whether her body was light or heavy, strong or weak. She would disappear.

Afterward, she often wondered why she failed to notice the black spaces in the film, the narrow bars that partitioned the frames. They must have filled ten percent of the reel, and yet she never caught so much as a glimpse of them. The people on screen appeared absolutely continuous—their faces, their gestures—though she knew that they were not. Perhaps the same was true of everybody. What if we flickered in and out of existence a hundred times a second, so quickly that no one could see it? What if our perception of an ongoing, coherent life was merely a trick of the eyes, an illusion born of our slowness of vision? This was how she had experienced life during her pregnancy with Celia, when every moment had seemed sweet and lagging and self-contained. It was a wonderful drowsing of time, and she and Christopher had lain together for hours some days pressing their hands to her stomach to feel for a turn or a kick. The question that worried her most was this: What would happen if the film snapped?

Happiness. A Simple Plan. Affliction. The Whole Wide World.

She rarely went to the movies at night and not at all during the weekend. She had never been the kind of person who could lose herself in crowds: she became, instead, all the more aware of herself, of where she began and ended, like a jigsaw piece clustered together with a thousand others. At night, then, she liked to stay home, cooking dinner and reading books and talking with Christopher when he wasn't sleeping or casting accusations against himself. It was only three or four times a year, when he hid himself away in the library, refusing to answer her voice, that she found herself driving to the theater after dark.

There was *The English Patient.*

There was *The Truman Show.*

There was *Rushmore* and *The Ice Storm* and *Dancer, Texas, Pop. 81.*

And there was *The Deep End of the Ocean,* with Michelle Pfeiffer and Treat Williams as the parents of a missing child—he was a boy, several years younger than Celia—and Whoopi Goldberg as the police detective assigned to their case. Janet did not know what the movie was going to be about when she bought her ticket, but even if she had, she probably would have stayed. There was a part of her that went to the movies to escape from her own life—she would never deny it—but there was another part, no less powerful or needy, that went to the movies to confront her life. She believed in sidelong glances, accidents of perspective, in the things we discover about ourselves when we think we're looking in another direction. (Could we ever, truly, look in another direction? She didn't know.) But, more than that, she would have stayed because she was lonely, and Christopher had sealed himself away in the library again with his books and his guilt, and the only other movie playing at the Reservoir Ten, or the only one she hadn't already seen, was some teen horror flick called *Idle Hands,* and she knew better than to try that.

It was a Friday night, and the theater was packed. She took the only aisle seat she could find, one row from the front, craning her neck so that she could see the screen, and she listened as the conversations around her faded to a whisper. After the commercials and the trailers, the light fell completely away for a moment, and then the Mandalay tiger appeared on screen, growling and padding toward the camera. At first everything was okay: Michelle Pfeiffer was loading her two sons into the car, driving through Wisconsin to her high school reunion, and Janet was watching with that same sudden loosening of her senses that she always felt in a darkened theater. It was not until they reached the crowded lobby of the hotel that she began to have her misgivings about the movie, and not until Michelle Pfeiffer went to register at the front desk, leaving the children to look after themselves, that she felt the first real stab of panic in her gut.

Of course one of the boys was missing when she returned—the younger one, only three years old—*of course* he was. And what Janet couldn't believe was that when she went to look for him, knocking her way through a roomful of arms and elbows, she left *the other one* behind. What was she thinking? Children melt away like frost in the sunlight: that's how easily they disappear. And Janet was sure it would happen to the older one as well, though in fact it did not.

There were thousands of stories about missing children, in books and movies and newspaper accounts, and in all of them, without exception, it was the mothers who lost possession of themselves, who stumbled and wailed and went coasting off into some terrible private silence. The fathers were the ones who held the world together, clasping the mothers to their chests and stroking their hair. They spoke to the police officers, answered the reporters, then put on their ties and went back to work. The fathers were heroes. The fathers were lions.

It was no surprise, then, when Michelle Pfeiffer buried herself in her bedroom while Treat Williams looked after their home and family, and as Janet looked on, a tiny space of resentment cracked open inside her, cool and empty like the hollow between two rocks. This was who she was supposed to be: this wispy, brittle woman, broken not by sorrow (the whole world was broken by sorrow) but by her failure to remember who she was. She hated it. The stories people told were all wrong. She kept repeating these words to herself, *It's all wrong, it's all wrong,* and felt the rift inside her opening wider and wider as Michelle Pfeiffer screamed at her husband and ignored her son and tunneled more deeply into her blankets. And then, nine years later, after she had healed and moved to another city, she found him, her missing child, living just two blocks away.

The boy came to the door offering to mow her lawn, and she recognized him immediately, surreptitiously snapping his picture to show the police. It was a fantasy, certainly—but a rich one, a commanding one—and for a few minutes Janet began to settle again into the movie. If children can vanish in a moment, she thought, leaving not a mark behind, then perhaps they can return in exactly the same way, every hair and every bone of them, simply and completely. She sank into the cushioning of her chair, watching as the boy moved back in with his family, leaving behind the man he had known as his father. Michelle Pfeiffer and Treat Williams welcomed the boy into their lives, and he stepped ever so cautiously closer, like a swimmer touching his toe to the water and wading in inch by inch. But he did not remember them, and he did not want to stay.

He wanted to return to his other home, he told them, to his father's home.

"There are worse things than being dead," he said.

Janet gave an audible gasp—she barely heard it at the time, but felt it afterward as a squeezing pinch in her throat. To return a child to his mother and to wrest him away again, or to allow him to wrest himself away, and then to say to that mother, *He isn't yours now, he belongs to someone else*, to say, *He never missed you*—she could not believe that anyone could be so merciless. A sour taste rose in her mouth, and she swallowed it back down. She felt like one of the very first moviegoers, those gentlemen in coats and ties who saw a train rushing into the camera and leapt from their seats braced for collision.

This is bullshit, she thought, *this is terrible,* and then she said it out loud. She couldn't help herself. "This is terrible."

Her voice was barely a murmur, and the only person who seemed to hear her was the man in the next seat, who shifted his popcorn to his other leg and made a breathy sound of disapproval, a *hush* amputated just before the *sh*.

She said it again, louder, "This is terrible," and this time it was not that she couldn't help herself, but that she didn't want to. She felt as though a hot steel wire were buzzing in her head. Her hands twisted at the fabric of her skirt. There was a titter from the two small boys in front of her, and someone behind her kicked at the spine of her chair.

The man sitting next to her said, "Do you want me to call the manager?" On screen Treat Williams and Michelle Pfeiffer were discovering that the son they had finally found had run away—he wasn't in his bedroom, he wasn't in the kitchen. "Because I will," the man declared.

Janet turned to him and, no longer bothering to muffle her voice, said, "It is, though. Pure bullshit. Can't you see that?" and she flailed her hand angrily at the screen.

From three or four points around the theater she heard the snakelike hiss of people trying to silence her. The man beside her said, "Look, *lady,* people here are trying to watch the movie," and another voice answered from a few rows behind, "Damn right we are."

"Fine." Janet rose into the aisle, fixing her purse around her shoulder. For a moment she truly thought she was going to leave. But then she heard Michelle Pfeiffer and Treat Williams arguing with each other—

"What are we gonna do now?"

"Don't push me on this, Beth."

"I want to give him back."

—and she stopped still. They were standing in their backyard, clouds streaming over the sun in a slow gray thread, leaves rustling in the grass. Treat Williams set his jaw, and Michelle Pfeiffer let her eyes flicker away for a moment, then met his gaze. Later Janet would wonder why she did it, but at the time she did not think to put the question to herself; perhaps she wanted to push back at the movie, or push her way into it (if she were living inside the movie she could bend it down a different path, a better one), or perhaps it was simply a pause on her way to the back exit. She was acting on instinct, and she did not pretend to know the reason why. What happened was this: she took a few steps forward and, raising her arm above her head, pressed her palm to the screen. It was pliant and glossy, like the thick integument of an eggplant, and she imagined that if she dug her nails in she could leave permanent moon-shaped impressions there. Her arm took on the green shade and tiny hitching motions of the grass where Michelle Pfeiffer and Treat Williams were standing.

She heard a chair retracting and turned to see the man who had been sitting next to her stamping out of the theater. "Will you move already?" somebody said, and she dropped her hand.

There was a low door beneath the screen, no higher than her chest, and she saw a chink between the jamb and the frame where it had not been properly locked. She ran her fingers along the crack, almost idly, as one might trace a line of condensation on a water glass, and the door floated open.

She ducked her head through to look inside.

It appeared to be some sort of storage chamber. There were

a few dusty boxes, a stack of empty film reels, and a tangled heap of black film that reminded her of the snarls of cassette tape she sometimes saw on the aprons of busy roads. She looked up a long wall of cinder blocks and saw the image of the missing boy reversed on the back of the screen. It filled the chamber with a light that shifted and jumped.

Though she had watched a thousand movies in this theater, and a hundred, probably, in this very room, she would never have known that such a space existed if she hadn't chanced upon it. How many people did, she wondered. An A-frame ladder stood open on the floor, and she stepped inside—again, she did not know why, and later she would not be able to explain it—and climbed one, two, three rungs, until she faced the back of the screen, then two more, until her legs lifted out of the shadows and the light covered her entirely. On Celia's fourth birthday, some three years before she vanished, she had scaled a ladder that a roofer had left leaning against the side of the house. It was during a game of hide-and-seek she was playing with her friends, and when she reached the highest rung, just beneath the rain gutter, she looked between her feet and froze rigid. Janet had to climb to the top and carry her back down, her scarecrow arms hooked tight around Janet's neck. When they hit the ground with a final hop, Celia said, "You *saved* my *life*, Mommy," and kissed her on the cheek, and then Robin Unwer tagged her and said, "You're it." That night, when Janet put Celia to bed, she complained that she could not sleep, and Janet believed she was witnessing the beginning of a phobia—that for the rest of her life her daughter would fall dizzy behind high windows, avoid railings and escalators, and refuse to cross bridges. Instead, and soon after, she headed straight in the other direction, climbing all the tallest structures she could find: jungle gyms, trees, the outer beams of the deck in the backyard. Standing on the ladder behind the movie screen, Janet thought she could understand why: when you rose into the air, even when nothing awaited you there, it always felt purposeful, like you were climbing *toward* something.

Michelle Pfeiffer was driving her son across the city in her car, and Janet could hear the thrum of the engine beneath their conversation, but she was too close to the screen to see where they were going. From where she stood they were giants—eyes as tall as doorways, lips as long as railroad ties. They could swallow her whole. A pencil of light was streaming through a hole in the screen, flickering against her shirt. She tried to plug it with her finger, but it was only wide enough to fit the sharp edge of her nail, which she twisted back and forth until it caught against a nick in the material.

A voice sounded from inside the theater. It was one of the boys in the front row. "I saw her. She crawled in there," he said, and a moment later Janet heard a rustling of bodies beneath her.

When she fit her nail to the corner of the notch, sliding it up as far as her arm could reach, the screen split open just like a zipper.

There was *East of Eden*, which she watched with her high school film club on the same afternoon they saw *The Kid from Left Field*, borrowing both movies from the town library when they learned that James Dean and Gary Coleman shared a birthday (February 8—that was the date). She remembered how James Dean slouched against the wall in the police station, and how he held a red handkerchief to his face to staunch the bleeding, and how when Burl Ives showed him a picture of his parents he swallowed his words and said, "I hate her, and I hate him, too." She did not remember much about *The Kid from Left Field*—only that she had seen it.

The school projector always sounded like a bicycle with a playing card pinned between the spokes, rattling softly and then loudly and then softly again, and it gave the movies they watched in the classroom a stuttering sort of rhythm, a cadence or music that lay just beneath the action and came to seem inseparable from it. Janet could hear this sound dimly in her head as she sat in the police station waiting to be processed, just an hour after the manager of the theater summoned a squad car to take her away. She spotted a streamer tied to a rotating fan, flickering in the air as the fan turned haltingly back and forth, and she listened to it growing louder as it swiveled toward her and weaker as it swiveled away, just like the projector at her high school.

No wonder these ancient movies were coming to mind.

The fan must have been new, she thought, chewing at the inside of her lip. She had never seen it before, and she had been in the police station many times these past two years, at least once a week since Celia.

Celia.

Her name—her simple, unembellished name—had become a shorthand for something else altogether: *the day Celia disappeared, and all the time since.* She used it the way she had once used *Christopher* to mean *when Christopher and I first started dating,* and later *when Christopher and I first got married,* the way she used *Oregon* to mean *the four years I spent in college.* She hated this change, hated the way it stripped her daughter's name of all its life and joy, but she found it impossible to weed it from her mind.

She had been in the waiting room for almost half an hour. The benches were made of a yellow fiberglass, and whenever she tried to adjust her posture she would lose her purchase and slip forward a few inches. The teenage couple on the bench across from her were having the same problem, and after a while they began to mug for each other—tobogganing to the very edge of the bench, throwing up their arms, and giggling. Janet watched them. The girl spread the fingers of her right hand open, tapping them one at a time and chanting, "Johnny, Johnny, Johnny, Johnny! Whoops, Johnny! Whoops, Johnny!" and the boy slipped forward in his seat again, and then they both folded over with laughter, hiding their faces behind a curtain of limp black hair. Slowly and fitfully they grew calm again, dropping into another chain of laughter every thirty seconds or so, two or three or four links long, and then sighing and falling quiet once more, and when they had finally exhausted themselves the girl cupped her hand around the boy's leg, and the boy rested his head on her shoulder, and they gave each other a lazy kiss.

Janet heard a door swinging open behind her, and a low voice, calming and ragged, a bartender's voice, said, "They told me I'd find you out here." It was Kimson Perry, the superintendent of the Springfield police force. He had been in charge of the local investigation of Celia's disappearance—*is*, Janet reminded herself, *is* in charge—and was a friend of hers, the contrabassoonist in the Community Orchestra where she played clarinet. He sat beside her and took her hand. "So what happened, Janet? Terry said they picked you up for destruction of property."

"I ripped the screen at the movie theater. It was almost an accident. I don't know." Only an hour ago the manager of the Reservoir Ten had coaxed her down from the ladder and into the sudden glaring brightness of the theater, where he announced to the patrons that the rest of this showing would have to be canceled—no, he couldn't refund their money, it was already locked away, but they could collect their free passes from the ushers as they left—and already it seemed like a dream to her. She was always so quiet at the movies, so retiring. The story was one she would never recognize herself in. When she was a girl her father liked to tell their dinner guests about the night her mother was in labor with her: a nurse, it seemed, had told her that it wasn't time to push yet, and her mother had coldcocked the nurse, knocking her flat. Afterward, her father said, when he tried to tell her what had happened, she wouldn't believe him. He laughed gigantically whenever he told this story, slapping the table with his palm, but Janet knew then—and she knew even more now—how her mother must have felt each time she heard it: surprised and embarrassed by what she had done, but with a fierce, rapacious wish to defend herself.

Kimson Perry gave a barely perceptible nod. "That's what I heard. Okay, Janet. I talked to the guy at the theater and explained your situation. Everyone's allowed to go crazy once, I told him. It took some doing, but he agreed with me. So this is your one and only close call. Your get-out-of-jail-free card, as it were."

"Thank you, Kimson."

"You're willing to pay the cost of repairs, of course?"

"Of course."

"Good." He let go of her hand. "We already have your prints on file from Celia, so you can take off as soon as you're ready. Have you called Christopher yet?" She shook her head. "Here, use my cell." He pulled the phone from his pocket, snapping it open so that the LCD monitor shone a cool, glacial green, and handed it over to her. "I'll be back for it in a few minutes. And I'll have a form or two we'll need for you to sign, okay?" He stood then, reflexively touching his holster, the way that men from small towns will check their back pockets for their wallets when they visit a big city, and after hovering awkwardly over her for a moment he said, "We haven't given up, you know."

For a long minute he looked into her face, trying to present a conviction he could not possibly feel, and then he left through the thick steel door. It closed behind him with a pneumatic hiss.

Janet knew that Christopher would not answer the phone. He was shut away in the library—sometimes pacing, sometimes standing silently, as always—and he would be there for the rest of the night. She would be surprised if he even remembered she was gone. Eventually he would fall asleep in his armchair, a green-shaded table lamp warming his lap, and when he woke in the morning he would shower and walk downstairs and cook his breakfast and pretend that everything was okay. Sometimes, late at night, when Janet stood outside the library door she would hear him talking to himself. It was a habit they shared— speaking out loud to themselves—never in a chatty or a conversational way, but almost subliminally, flinging individual sentences into the air in response to the discussions they were having with themselves in their heads. Janet did it only to reassure herself, she had found: *It will be okay*, she would catch herself saying, or *Don't you worry*. But when she listened to Christopher he always seemed to be accusing himself in a rage. *Stupid, stupid. I can't believe it. No. No. It was all your fault.* Before Celia disappeared, they had spoken about having a second child—another girl, they hoped—but now they both found the idea horrifying. Especially Christopher. At breakfast one morning he had erupted with laughter—his own first laughter—when he found an Associated Press article about a man who had drowned after jumping from a 140-foot bridge into a harbor on a dare from his drinking buddies. He read the final sentence of the article aloud, "He told them he'd leaped from higher elevations," then laughed again and handed the paper to Janet, creased beneath the last paragraph. The headline was MAN SHOUTS "YAHOO," LEAPS TO DEATH.

As she dialed her home number, she pictured Christopher in the library. He would be staring out the window, pressing his forehead to the glass and then wiping away the spot of oil he had left, or collapsing into his armchair, waiting for the light to resume. Though she knew he was not listening, she left a message for him on the answering machine: "This is Janet, Christopher. Something's happened, and I'm at the police station. Don't worry, I'm okay, but I need you to come and get me. My car is still at the movies, and I need a ride. Are you there, Christopher? Pick up the phone if you're listening. Hello. Hello. It isn't Celia, nothing's happened with Celia. Are you there? Come on, Christopher." She looked around the waiting room—at the clock behind the wire grille, at the old nicked ashtray beneath the new NO SMOKING sign, at the boy and girl on the other bench. "All right. I'll try you again in a little while," she said, and she switched the phone off.

She shut her eyes, massaging them delicately with her index fingers, but they soon began to sting, and when she opened them again she saw two distinct, overlapping images of the room, which drifted slowly toward the center of her vision before they locked back together. The girl and the boy on the other bench were staring at her as though she had in fact split apart, cracking like a walnut into two separate pieces, viewing the world by a difference of inches. The girl said, "I just figured out where I recognize you from."

Janet dropped a lazy, "Oh?" She knew what was coming. *You're that woman, that mother,* the girl would say, *the one I saw on the news, the one whose daughter went up like a puff of smoke.* She had heard it so many times before that the words took on strange echoes in her head. *That woman, that mother, another mother, another lover. A puff of smoke, a cloud of dust, and a hearty heigh-ho-silver.* It was like the gabbling of voices she sometimes heard between radio stations, and she wished she could shut it off.

But the girl surprised her. She did not mention Celia. Perhaps she had never even heard of her. Instead she said, "You play with the Community Orchestra. Clarinet, right?"

"That's right," Janet said.

"I thought so. I play clarinet at my high school." The boy, who was trailing his finger idly up and down the seam of her blue jeans, worked his mouth beneath the collar of her shirt and kissed her neck. She closed her eyes and gave a slow *mmm* of pleasure. Then she nudged him away and said, "Pierre plays oboe." She leaned toward Janet and whispered conspiratorially, "And you ripped the screen at the movie theater? Really?"

"I did," said Janet.

"Kick ass. Which movie?"

She felt a smile quirk her lips. *"Deep End of the Ocean."*

The boy interrupted her: "Whoopi Goldberg." He tossed his hair back from his forehead. "No eyebrows. Lady trips me out."

The girl tucked a loose strand of hair behind her ear. "We're here for breaking and entering," she said.

"And theft," said the boy.

"Breaking and entering and theft," the girl confirmed.

It was neither a boast nor a confession, but seemed to contain something of each. "What did you steal?" Janet asked.

The girl squeezed the boy's hand. "Electronics components—television, computer, and stereo. The individual parts are worth more than the machines, it turns out. So what we did was we broke into people's houses, opened the machines, and just took the parts we wanted. Then we put everything back together. It worked just fine until tonight."

"I don't understand. You only took the *parts?*"

"Yeah. Like I said, we could get more money that way."

The boy nodded. "We know this guy."

"But if all you want is one part or another, why not take the whole machine and then strip it down later? Wouldn't that be quicker?"

"That's what *I* argued," the girl said. She was running her finger around the outside of the boy's ear, slowly, as though trying to draw a sustained note from the rim of a glass. "But Pierre wouldn't do it."

"Funnier that way," the boy said. "Picture all these people calling their repairmen, and the repairmen show up and they find nothing but these hollow shells waiting for them. 'What is this, a joke, lady? You're missing your motherboard here.' This happens fifty or sixty times all over town, and suddenly nobody knows what to think anymore."

Janet tried to imagine the situation as the boy did, with the same air of harmless mischief, but she could not. Instead she saw only the people whose houses they had broken into. She thought of their faces when they discovered that something else was missing or broken in their home, something else had gone unaccountably wrong. Her conception of what other people were capable of shrugging off or accepting as part of the natural absurdity of the world had been forever altered by the loss of her daughter. You could not presume that people were healthy. You could not presume that they would welcome the little nudges and jostlings of life. You had to behave as though everyone you met was walking a thin wire far above the earth, where the slightest wind might rock them off their balance and send them tumbling to the ground. This was how you had to live if you wanted to be careful.

"Anyway," the boy said, "that was the idea."

The girl pressed firmly against his ankle with the toe of her shoe. "He's a real expert when it comes to electronics. I mean, you wouldn't believe it. He can take a machine apart and put it back together just like that." She kissed him again, on the cheek, and he smiled and dropped his head and let his hair sweep back over his eyes.

Then Kimson Perry returned from his office and they both fell silent, shrinking into their jackets like two mice hiding in a hummock of leaves.

Kimson bent over Janet and asked, "So did you find Christopher?"

"Not yet." She passed him the phone. "I thought I would try him again in a few minutes. Either that or call a cab."

He gestured at the boy and the girl. "Let me have ten minutes with these two, and I can give you a ride myself."

She nodded. "Thanks."

"Good," he said, and he handed her a slip of paper with three separate leaves—one white, one red, and one yellow. "Read this over and sign your name by the cross. It's for the incident report. Nothing unusual," and he made a beckoning motion to the teenagers on the bench. "Come on, you two. Follow me."

As they passed beside her, Janet saw the girl mouthing something to the boy—she could not distinguish the words—and the boy shrugged and shook his head. His left ear was a bright, wind-bitten red where she had been stroking it with her finger. He spidered his hand into the back pocket of her blue jeans.

The door drifted smoothly shut behind them, locking in place with a final tug of the pneumatic rod.

After Janet signed the document Kimson had given her—an account of "the incident" in the Reservoir Ten, along with a statement that she, "the perpetrator," had agreed to pay any and all damages to the owner—she began to feel a rawness in her throat like the stab of a needle. There was a watercooler beneath the bulletin board at the other end of the waiting room, and, though she recognized the danger, she decided to risk a drink. She had been avoiding the bulletin board ever since she had come to the police station, letting her eyes skip away from it to the clock or the floor or the ceiling tiles so that she would not have to read the latest HAVE YOU SEEN THIS CHILD? poster:

NAME: CELIA BROOKS
AGE: 9
DATE OF BIRTH: 12/06/89
MISSING SINCE: 03/15/97

She knew that if she allowed herself she would sink into those statistics like a stone—it had certainly happened before—so she did not permit herself to see them at all. She had found that she could do this: place a darkened slide over one section of a room or one paragraph of a book and simply refuse to perceive it, the way she could examine her face in the mirror without ever looking into her eyes.

She searched for a cup by the watercooler and found a stacked column of them in the cabinet underneath. When she pressed the tap, the water trickled into the cup in two thin strands that joined and spindled about each other, and as she drank and filled her cup and drank again she remembered the orchestra rehearsal she had attended on the day that Celia vanished. It had something to do with the sound the water made, which reminded her of a song Celia had learned in kindergarten: "The clarinet / the clarinet / plays doodle-doodle-doodle-doodle-det"—a line that, even the first time she heard it, sounded to her more like the pattering of water than it did like the clarinet.

The Springfield Community Orchestra rehearsed every Saturday at the Holy Souls Catholic Assembly Hall, a weathered brick building with a long sloping gallery and arched wooden rafters. She had called Christopher midway through the session that day, while the conductor was practicing with the strings, and he had said that Celia was playing outside, and she had asked him if he wanted her to pick anything up at the grocery store, and he had said hamburger buns and paper towels, and then, when she told him to take care, he had answered, "I always do." Or had that been earlier? The orchestra was preparing a Menotti ballet for their spring performance, and as she hung up she had heard the violins playing a few light bars of an arietta. By the time she drove home that afternoon, Celia was already missing.

Though she thought, in the weeks and months afterward, about leaving the orchestra, she did not. Instead, she held tight to it. She found the music—she found losing herself in it—a comfort, and it had been more than a year now since she had missed a rehearsal. In three months they would perform their annual summer pops concert, a program of songs from classic motion pictures, and she allowed some of the tunes to drift through her head: "As Time Goes By" from *Casablanca*, "In the Cool, Cool, Cool of the Evening" from *Here Comes the Groom*, "The Wishing Well Song" from *Snow White and the Seven Dwarfs*.

Snow White and the Seven Dwarfs. It was the first movie Janet took Celia to see in the theater. She was only two years old at the time, and within five minutes she had taken her sandals off and stepped onto Janet's lap to get a better view of the screen. She laughed each time Dopey appeared, giving a rigid little hop that made Janet grasp her beneath the arms to steady her, but she had nightmares for months about the Wicked Queen. Years later she told Janet that when she said her prayers at night, she always imagined the Queen dipping her red apple into the vat of poison at the phrase "God deliver us from evil."

The last movie Janet saw with Celia was *Matilda*, with Mara Wilson as Matilda and Danny DeVito and Rhea Perlman as her parents. It was based on Celia's favorite Roald Dahl book, which her father had read to her the month before she started school and which she herself, a precocious reader, had read three times since. The first paragraph was one of the most biting Janet had ever heard: "It's a funny thing about mothers and fathers. Even when their own child is the most disgusting little blister you could ever imagine, they still think that he or she is wonderful," and each time Celia finished the book, she took to calling her friends "blisters" for a few weeks whenever she argued with them. The movie was delightful—agile, irreverent, almost glowing with life—and after it ended the two of them went out for ice cream. They did not make it home until late that evening, when the sun was just a faint gleam of silver behind the darkest blue of the sky. Christopher was waiting on the porch when they pulled into the driveway. He said that he had been worried about them.

The cooler released a tremendous bubble that broke through the water with a hiccuping noise and then shuddered apart at the surface, and Janet came blinking up out of her memories. She tossed her cup into the trash. She was just about to return to her seat when she heard footsteps clapping across the police station. Along the front of the waiting room was a glass wall with a sheet of wire netting inside that looked out onto the lobby, and from there to the sidewalk and the front curb. A black woman, shaking with nervous emotion, ran across the floor to the reception desk. She was calling the question that Janet had heard herself calling two years before, the question that all mothers call in their hearts: "Where's my daughter? Where's my daughter?" A police officer asked her for her name, then said, "Calm down, ma'am. We've got her in back," and escorted her around the corner and out of sight. Janet listened as their footsteps faded away.

She felt a tightness in her hands, a stinging pressure in the joints of her fingers, and when she looked down she found that she was kneading them like heavy lumps of modeling clay. She let go, flexing them one at a time in the air until they stopped tingling. Then she took another cup from beneath the water-cooler and poured herself a second drink of water, which she tossed down in two swallows.

She threw the cup away and then carefully, reflexively, wiped her fingerprint from the watercooler's spout, using the tail of her shirt. Ever since she was a little girl, when she saw her first detective movie, she had been more than casually aware of where she left her fingerprints. It was a fixation that only became stronger in police stations and court buildings, hospitals and banks—places with hard, glossy surfaces where she felt dwarfed by the mechanisms of power. She remembered watching Basil Rathbone (or was it some later Sherlock Holmes?) dusting a glass with white powder and a tiny sweeper, then blowing gently to reveal the whorl of the criminal's fingerprint, and she remembered, too, the surprise she felt as she realized for the first time that she left a record of herself in everything she touched—that nothing she did, nothing anybody did, could ever escape the world's notice.

It was not true, of course. She knew that now. There were some events, events beyond number, that left no record in the world at all. But still, whenever she was in a police station, she always tried to rub her fingerprints away. She couldn't break the habit.

She took her seat on the bench and listened to the people shuffling by in the corridor, to the clock ticking on the wall, to the streamer flickering from the rotating fan, and it was only a few minutes before the steel door wheeled open and Kimson Perry came out, the boy and the girl trailing quietly behind him. The sleeves of their jackets were gathered at their elbows. Their fingertips were spiraled with ink.

Kimson cleared his throat with a small interrogative cough. "Can you give me just one more minute with these two, Janet? I promised their parents I'd wait for them. It shouldn't be too long."

"Of course." She held out the statement she had signed. "Do you want this?"

"Oh, right. The F-11. Let me go slip that in your file," he said, and with a few short taps of his shoes he was gone again.

The girl dropped heavily onto the bench across from Janet. "This sucks," she said, lightly taking hold of the boy's jacket.

"Sucks indeed," the boy answered, and he reached into his pocket and came up with a gray bandanna. He walked to the watercooler and doused it through, waiting for the color to deepen, then sat beside the girl and began wiping the ink from her fingers, delicately, one by one, blowing each finger dry when he was finished.

"Not only do our parents know all about the houses now,"

the girl said, and she shut her eyes, "but we're going to have to tell them why we did it. You realize that, don't you?"

"I do," the boy said, and Janet watched him lay her first hand aside and start on the second. He looked as though he were cleaning an antique satin doll, or a bird that had just hatched from its egg, something infinitely soft and fragile.

"Why *did* you do it?" Janet asked.

The girl opened her eyes. "We're not just some bored juvenile delinquents if that's what you're thinking. But, well, we're going to be needing the extra money soon—aren't we, Pierre?"

At that she opened her free hand and pressed it gently, deliberately, to her stomach.

A smile lifted into the boy's cheeks, and he nodded.

Janet heard an involuntary *oh* slip from her mouth, a quick little gasp of surprise and sadness and trepidation, muddled together with the strangest envy. She felt suddenly as though she had become the girl's mother, or even the girl herself, as though she were playing her in a movie while a hundred spectators watched from the audience, and she wondered what she was going to say next.

"You're going to be a mother?" she asked.

"Uh-huh."

"But you're so—young," Janet said.

A ticking stillness filled the room. The girl's mouth twitched and her eyes began to glass over—from sadness or joy or exhaustion, or some other, nameless emotion—and the boy touched the bandanna to her cheek, leaving a lash-shaped mark of gray ink there. "I know," she said, her voice all but toneless. Janet could not tell what she was feeling until she gave a short breath of what sounded like laughter. Then she shook her head, declaring, "I'm not supposed to be happy about this, am I? But I can't help it," and she laughed again, more clearly this time.

She kissed the boy. "Happy, happy, happy," she whispered, and the boy whispered something back, something indistinguishable, that made the girl grin.

Janet felt an unexpected lightening inside her. There was no behavior so outlandish that it wasn't a believable human response to the world. She heard the steel door opening behind her and looked up to see Kimson standing over her shoulder, but before he could interrupt, she turned back to the girl. "But what are your parents going to say?" she asked her.

"Well, *my* folks aren't too bad," the girl said. "But Pierre—" She realized it all at once. "Oh my God! Pierre, your father is going to kill you."

The boy lifted one shoulder, a nervous shrug that almost touched his ear. "I know. He's on his way right now. I just called him."

And at that moment a car rattled to a stop outside the station. They heard the door slam at the curb—all four of them—and they turned to look. But it was not the boy's father. Janet recognized the car. It was her husband arriving, out of his silence and out of his grief, to take her home.

The Ghost of Travis Worley

The trouble is they don't know they're dead.

They hang around. The kindest thing to do
if you should ever see one is simply to say,
"Listen, you're dead. You're dead. Get out of here."
That's what the ghost eventually will do

when we've told it again and again to go.
"Get out of here. Get out of here. You're dead."
They can't of course go anywhere on purpose;
you have to give them intent to make them go.

And who knows where?

—MILLER WILLIAMS

Sometimes I remember my friends and family so clearly it's as if I'm looking down at them through a flawless lens of water, the kind that lay over our pond on those quiet spring mornings after nights of heavy rain, but the vision never seems to last for long. Something inside me always shifts or gives way, and a fog of silt spreads through the water, and one by one they disappear. My mom and my dad. My best friend Kristen Lanzetta. My other friends Robin Unwer and Oscar Martin and Andrea Onopa. And the new kid, whose name we could never remember, or maybe he just never told us, so that after a while we simply gave up and called him Kid: "Hey, Kid, why don't you play goalie for us?" "Did anybody see where the Kid went?"

They waver and darken, the people I knew. They hide away from me and step into the light.

I remember playing in my front yard one winter afternoon with Oscar Martin and Kristen Lanzetta. Kick the Can. The Lion King. Bubblegum, Bubblegum. The sun was out, but we could feel the wind cutting at us as the cars passed by, and there were places in the shade where needles of ice still floated in the puddles. The last of the snow was melting from the gutters into pockets of wet black grit, and in another day or two it would be completely gone. Kristen and I had on our matching purple jackets and gloves, the ones our mothers had bought for us before the school year started, and which we had been so excited to wear—we would look *exactly the same, like sisters*—that we began carrying them to school with us at the very first hint of cold weather.

This is how sharply I see everything before it begins to fade away.

Kristen and Oscar and I were tossing a tennis ball to each other, swinging at it with Oscar's red plastic bat, when we caught sight of the new kid watching us from beneath the maple trees at the side yard of the house (there were two of them there, and an elm tree, their branches fanning out above a crumbling stone wall). He was rocking his sister back and forth in the ancient hoodless baby carriage he always wheeled her around in, and she was watching him through her deep blue eyes, her hands opening and closing at her shoulder. She was a tiny thing, always perfectly quiet, so small that she might have nestled comfortably, squirrel-like, inside a Kleenex box. Every time I saw her this was the image that came to my mind.

"Hey, we're playing baseball. You want to pitch?" I called out to Kid. He came over and took the ball from me. "I'm good at this game," he said, and he was. He gave a few arcing tosses which Kristen sent thumping against the wall of the house and Oscar and I swung at and missed, swung at and missed. Then we offered him the bat. He couldn't seem to get a grip on it. It kept bouncing out of his hands to the ground.

"Wait a second," he told us, and he gave a hitching run over to the stone wall where he had left his baby sister, coming back with a long stick that had fallen from the maple tree. "Can I use this instead?" he asked, and when he crouched over the pizza box we were using for a plate and Oscar pitched him the ball, saying, "Let's see you try and hit this one," he snapped his arm around the way a cat bats at its reflection in the water, and the ball sailed off the side of the house and came tumbling back over our heads.

We watched it land across the street.

"He who hits it, gets it," Oscar said, angry that Kid had connected with the ball. He made a gesture with his thumb. "And that's you, Limpy."

Kristen had come home from school with me to spend the night, so it must have been a Friday afternoon. Cars and trucks and SUVs were barreling by on their way home from work, but Kid acted as though he didn't see them at all. He dropped the stick and walked into the street and then across it, and he collected the tennis ball from Enid Embry's thornbushes, holding it up so that it glowed like a yellow apple in the sunlight. Then he stepped off the curb and walked straight into the path of a minivan.

I screwed my eyes shut and listened for the shriek of tires, for the smack of his body as it rolled up the hood. But when I looked again he was standing safely in my own front yard. He gave the ball to me and tucked his hand in his pocket. The minivan was at the other end of the street, waiting its turn at the stop sign, as peaceful as a cow chewing grass.

"Holy crap," I heard Kristen say, "I thought you were dead for sure."

And then—

Then it happens. Once again I turn my head, or I try to reach out for them, and they dissolve in a ripple of sparks.

I cannot see them.

I do not know where they've gone.

When my vision clears again (it would be impossible for me to say how much time has passed: minutes? years?), I see myself cleaning out the refrigerator in our kitchen. This was one of my chores, back when I was a girl. I had to clean the refrigerator, and keep my bedroom tidy, and empty the small bathroom trash cans into the big kitchen trash can. I had to borrow sugar or milk or flour from Enid Embry or Sara Cadwallader, our neighbors, and return their Tupperware to them when we were finished. And then there were the chores that Kristen Lanzetta and I invented for ourselves, a different one nearly every day, chores we carried out with an almost religious fussiness. We had to touch our elbows whenever someone said our name. We had to wear our matching yellow socks, the ones with the ducks on them, inside-out to school. We could not step on cracks, including the cracks that separated the panels of the sidewalk. We could not walk in the shade one day, or on the grass the next, or in the sunlight the next.

I was waiting for Kristen to knock on the door while I sorted through the refrigerator. It was Sunday morning, a week or so after the ice had melted from the puddles. Kristen was going to spend the day with me. Her mom and dad had promised to drop her off on their way to the movies.

Our refrigerator had a lazy motor, so that the food decayed much more quickly than it should have. I had to poke through it once a week (and every day during the summer) looking for signs of mold and rot. I checked fruits and vegetables for circles of gray fuzz. I opened milk bottles and containers of soup, sniffing for the sweet, sickly smell of spoilage. I was worried that Kristen would get there before I was finished. I had a secret I wanted to tell her—only her, my best friend—and I could feel it pushing like an enormous bubble against the back of my throat. My dad was at the stove, layering cheese and tuna and spinach into a casserole, and when I asked him if I had to clean the whole refrigerator right then, if I couldn't wait to do half of it tomorrow, he said that *when he was my age he had to walk five miles through the ice and snow to clean his refrigerator, and afterward he spent the whole day chopping logs and digging holes and throwing the logs he had chopped into the holes he had dug.*

"Yes, you have to do the whole thing," he said. He squeezed the back of my neck. "If Kristen gets here before you're finished, I'm sure she'll wait for you."

The air in the refrigerator was only medium-cool, contained in a single, solid block that I could barely even feel on my skin, and I looked through the food shelf by shelf, listening all the while for Kristen's car to purr to a stop in our driveway. The secret I wanted to tell her was this: *I had a dream last night that Oscar Martin asked me if he could be my boyfriend, and I told him yes, and he kissed me on the lips.* These were the exact words I was going to use.

I held a container of peaches to the window, watching the sun strike the syrup. I thought I saw Kid for a moment—he was standing by the pond in my backyard, just behind the line of elm trees, steadying his sister against his chest with his palm—but when I looked again he wasn't there. I put the peaches back on the shelf.

"This is all I found," I said to my dad, and I showed him a plate of sliced cheeses that had hardened to a pale crust at the edges. "Do you want me to throw them away?"

He took the plate from me and peeled the cling wrap off. When he caught the odor, he gave a grimace of such honest disgust that I couldn't keep from laughing. "Good Lord!" he said, and he replaced the cling wrap. "Here, throw the whole plate away. I can't imagine we'll want to use it again after this." He looked at the refrigerator and shook his head. "Ever. What's wrong with that thing, anyway?"

"I heard that," my mom said. She was coming down the winding wooden staircase that joined our kitchen to the rooms above, which always reminded me of the corkscrew my dad kept by the wine rack—I thought of it as an elaborate toy, with arms that could rise and fall in jumping jacks, but it was never as much fun to play with as I hoped it would be.

"What happened this time?" my mom asked, and my dad said, "We had a cheese fiasco."

She took the plate from me. "You know I'm ready to replace that thing just as soon as you are, Christopher. All you have to do is say the word."

He sprinkled some bread crumbs onto the casserole and shrugged his shoulders. "Let's give it a few more weeks to get its act together."

"You're the boss," she said. She turned to the refrigerator. "You hear that? You've been granted a stay of execution. I suggest you make the most of it." She scraped the cheese into the trash can and shut the lid.

A car turned off the street, and I heard its engine powering down though not switching off in our driveway. The sound shifted unmistakably, the way that water pouring from a faucet will change its pitch as it grows warmer or colder. A few seconds later there was a knock on the front door.

"See, finished in the nick of time," my dad said to me, but I was barely listening. I ran for the living room, past the staircase and the television and the decorative glass table, through the front room and into the foyer. I could feel the words popping open inside me: *I had a dream last night that Oscar Martin asked me if he could be my boyfriend, and I said yes, and he kissed me on the lips. You can't tell anyone else, okay? It's just between you and me. Promise you won't tell anyone, okay, Kristen? I had a dream last night that* . . .

But when I opened the door—and I can already see the moment shrinking away, consuming itself as I watch—Kristen was waiting there for me with Robin Unwer and Andrea Onopa. Each of them was wearing a clear plastic bracelet made of identical diamond-shaped beads. Kristen held hers out for me to see.

"We got them at the grocery store last night," she said. "Aren't they beautiful? Robin and Andrea spent the night with me, and I told them they could come over today. It's more fun this way, don't you think? With all four of us instead of just the two? You don't mind, do you, Celia? Do you?"

Another episode: Kid and I were playing on the wooden deck behind my house, jumping to the ground from the long, rickety incline of the staircase. Each time we landed we would climb one step higher and leap again, first him and then me. So far we had made it to the eighth stair. "Eight's my record," I told him. "Any higher and I chicken out," and he looked at me, and looked at the staircase, and then looked at me again, and said, "I bet we can do nine if we try it together."

I was doubtful. "If you think so . . ."

"I do." And so I followed behind him, counting off the steps. We lined up at the very edge of the ninth stair, leaning out over the drop. My legs went weak on me, soft and quivery. I felt like they would slide out from under me like a pair of soupy eggs. "I don't know about this," I said. "Are you sure we—"

"On the count of three," Kid interrupted, "One, two"—and just before we jumped, he took my hand—"three."

As we fell through the air everything seemed to vanish for a moment—the trees, the house, even my own body—but then, abruptly, it all came back. I had let go of Kid's hand, but I could still see him beside me. The stairs were rising up to meet us as they dropped away toward the ground. I felt the wind prickling against my scalp like a cloud of gnats. We landed hard.

I brushed the grass off my knees and stood up. "We did it!" I yelled. "We broke the record!"

Kid opened his mouth to answer, but a jet plane was passing overhead with a high thunder that grew louder and louder, and I couldn't tell what he was saying. He kept talking as though he didn't notice the plane at all. After the noise fell away, I asked him, "What was that? I didn't hear you."

"I said I'm hungry." He gave me a strange look and shook his head. "You need to get your ears checked."

"Come on, then, if you're hungry," I told him, and he followed me with his halting walk into the kitchen.

I decided that we should fix sandwiches. "I'll get the peanut butter and jelly ready, and you can make the toast," I said. "Okay?" and I laid the bread out on the counter. The jelly was inside the door of the refrigerator, but the peanut butter was tucked deep in the top shelf of the cabinet, and I had to stand on a chair I pulled over from the kitchen table to fish it out. I worked the jar open with both hands and then towed the chair back to the table. When I finished I saw that Kid was browning the bread inside the oven. I laughed. "Why didn't you just use the toaster?" I said.

"The toaster?"

"Of course the toaster. Here." But when I showed it to him, depressing the lever with its flattened-out rasping noise, he diverted his eyes.

"I—I don't know how to use that kind," he said, and he slipped an oven mitt onto his hand and collected the toast off the rack.

We were eating our sandwiches when I realized something. "Hey, where's your sister? I think this is the first time I've seen you without her."

He stared into the middle distance for five seconds, ten seconds, twenty, and then dropped the bread crust onto his paper towel, a look of shock washing over his face. His skin was turning the same translucent white as candle wax. "My sister!" he said, and he pushed his chair from the table and turned his head from me and—

And another: It was Oscar Martin's birthday, and there were ten or twelve of us huddled around the coffee table in his living room, watching as he opened his presents. A Nerf football. A bicycle helmet. An X-wing Fighter video game. I had given him a SuperSoaker water rifle, the kind with the extra storage tank which he had told me he wanted the summer before, rattling on about it whenever our parents took us to the swimming pool: "Man, I wish I had one of those! Nobody could stop me! I'd be invincible! G-doosh!" But one of his aunts, it turned out, had given him one for Christmas, and so, apparently, had one of his uncles, and when he opened it he rolled his eyes and showed it to his mom. "Well, that makes three," he said, and then: "Oh, yeah. Thanks, Celia."

After he had opened his presents, during those few shuffling minutes when we were still waiting to see what would happen next, I watched Kristen Lanzetta and Robin Unwer and Andrea Onopa touch their fingertips together in a pyramid and say, "Wonder Twin powers, *activate!*" They were the only other girls at the party. I recognized the slogan from a superhero cartoon, and even though I hated superheroes, I asked, "Can I be a Wonder Twin, too?"

"Sorry," said Andrea, and she rattled the beads on her wrist. "You have to have one of the Wonder Twin bracelets."

Kristen nodded. "Those are the rules. We can make you our pet monkey, though. Do you want to be our pet monkey?"

I shook my head and looked away. Oscar was tossing his Nerf football into the air and trying to catch it as it fell, but it kept tapping the light fixture and angling off to the side, bobbling around in a heap of wrapping paper and bows and Dixie cups stained with fruit punch. Kid was sitting with his back to the television and paging through one of Oscar's comic books while his sister slept beside him in her baby carriage. A cartoon was playing, filling the space around his body with a toneless white light. Finally Oscar's mother said, "Oscar, why don't you kids play one of the games we talked about?" and Oscar dropped his football and said, "Oh yeah. I forgot what came next," and announced, "Okay, guys, now we play Stoneface."

The rules were simple: two of us would stand eye to eye

with blank expressions on our faces, and we would try to keep from laughing. The first to crack a smile was the loser. I was going to ask Kristen to be my partner, but before I got the chance she had paired up with Robin Unwer, and Oscar Martin had paired up with David Kuperman, and Andrea Onopa had paired up with William Miller. Kid and I were the only two players left, and though he said he didn't want to play, he wanted to keep reading his comic book—"Just staring at someone like that . . . I don't know, I just don't like it"—I convinced him to join me anyway.

I had played Stoneface before and I knew that the trick was to look directly at one of his eyes—*at,* not *into*—which would dull the expression on his face; otherwise his personality would come teasing and flickering out of him like a flame from under a carpet and I would laugh almost immediately. Also, if I tried to keep a watch on *both* his eyes, or, even worse, on his whole face, I would start to feel my own eyes looking back at me, my own cheeks stretching helplessly into a smile, and I would not be able to stop myself. Within half a minute I found myself laughing anyway, but for the first few seconds I was staring at Kid, I could see a reflection of the room in his right eye, or patches of the room at least—the table, the walls, and the window, but not the VCR or the television; the bookshelves and the carpet, but not the stereo or the artificial houseplant.

When the final round of the game was finished, Oscar gave a box of chocolate-covered cherries to the winner. "Here's your prize, David, so eat it." Then he clapped his hands and said, "All right, our next game is going to be Scavenger Hunt. Everybody needs to pick a teammate, and then I'll hand out the instructions."

I tugged at the sleeve of Kristen's purple jacket. "Do you want to try this one together?" I asked.

"Well, I promised Robin I would do everything with her today. But maybe Andrea will be your partner."

"But Robin was with you last time! It's not fair," I said. "How come you never—"

But she interrupted me: "We can't be partners all the time, you know, Celia," and she shook her head and took Robin's hand and said to her, "See, it's just like I told you. Every single minute of the day."

I felt a stinging in my eyes, a pulsing heat, and I blinked a few times.

I—

I cannot remember where I was or what I did, how I felt or what I said.

Sometimes I close my eyes, and they all come back to me, my friends and family, not as the people they were in this particular moment or another, when they shared in my life, but in a bundle of their own quirks and habits and eccentricities, as closely connected as a cluster of blackberries. All I have to do is think of them by name.

My mom, for instance—who played the clarinet, and who would press the bell against my stomach when she came to tuck me in at night, blowing a warm buzz of air through the pipe that made me giggle and twist and squirm. She wore blue jeans and a sweater around the house—or, in the summer, blue jeans and a T-shirt—but occasionally, when we went out to eat, she would wear a wonderful sheer crinkly skirt that made a swishing sound when she walked that I liked to pretend was the ocean, rolling in and away, in and away. She kept a small, square vegetable garden filled with carrots and tomatoes and lettuce. She sang along to the music on the radio, and she always seemed to know all the words. Whenever she heard me talking with my friends about Oscar Martin or William Miller or John Pelevin, she would tell us that we were all *boy crazy.*

Kristen Lanzetta—who had long black hair that had never been cut, *never once, in all her life,* and which she pinned together in the back with a brown and yellow butterfly clip that was shaped like an actual butterfly. I had been friends with her ever since I was a baby, and we knew all the same stories and liked all the same people and invented hiding games, clapping and rhyming games, pony-riding games. She had a collection of plastic rings from the gum machine at the grocery store, and so did I, and we liked to trade them with each other on rainy days: her ruby ring for my diamond, my sapphire for her emerald. She had a cat, Simon, who hated both of us.

Oscar Martin—who was not only in my class at school but who also lived down the street from me, so that he came over to play with me sometimes even though I was a girl. He had wide clear green eyes, with a comma-shaped flaw of blue in the left one, and in the dream I had, when he kissed me on the lips, his breath had tasted like vanilla wafers. He was the fastest boy in the first grade, and on Track and Field Day he had won three separate races, one of them against the second- and third-graders. When there were no adults around he used words like *"damn"* and *"hell"* and *"sucks,"* and once I had even heard him say *"bitch."* He was the most popular boy in our class.

Robin Unwer—who put stickers of unicorns on all her notebooks, and was allergic to peanuts and bee stings, and had a swimming-pool-sized trampoline in her backyard. She liked to ice-skate, and whenever she was in my house she would take her shoes off and slide across the long kitchen floor in only her ankle socks. Sometimes, and more and more often, I saw her whispering at recess with Kristen Lanzetta.

Kid—who wore dark blue denim overalls and a white button-up shirt, the sleeves of which he rolled to his elbows, and whose sister wore a loose pink sleeper that looked like a pillowcase. He said that he had been living in our neighborhood *as long as he could remember,* though we had only met him recently, and he moved about so quietly that we never saw him coming or going: he was either there or he wasn't, like a light switch with only two settings. He walked with a limp in his right leg from a disease he had had when he was smaller—it was not the chicken pox, and it was not the measles, but something I had never heard of called polio, and he was worried that his baby sister was going to catch it, too. I never learned his name.

And there was, of course, *my dad*—who liked to cook and read and stare out the window. Whenever I complained about my chores, he would make up stories about the hardships of his childhood: *When I was your age I had to take fourteen naps a day, one every hour until it was time for me to go to bed,* or: *When I was your age I ate nothing but creamed corn, bowl after bowl of it, and if I didn't finish every single bite, I would have to take a bath in whatever was left.* He had broken his arm once, before I was born. He sometimes got headaches. He did not know how to whistle. In the evening he stood talking on the lawn with the real people who were our neighbors, and in the morning he wrote books filled with the imaginary ones who lived only in his head, and at times I think that if I wish or pray or concentrate hard enough, I will be able to tell my story through his hands.

When they disappear, and they always do, I imagine that a thick gray mist has surrounded me, rising from the ground in a thousand ribbons, and I can no longer see them through the haze. I might just as well imagine the opposite—that I am waiting in a park, the sun beating down on my shoulders, and they have run behind a hill or a stand of trees, chasing a leaf of paper that has just now caught the wind. I watched them go, and they will be right back. I could call to them, and I'm certain they would hear me.

There is little to do here but watch and remember.

The day before everything changed began as one of those late winter mornings where the first touch of sunlight melts the frost from the grass and became, as the sun lengthened and took the sky, one of those early spring afternoons where the wind carries the sound of a thousand birds.

It was recess, and I was kicking a trench into the gravel by the merry-go-round, waiting for my turn on the swingset. The older kids were all playing soccer in the parking lot, and around me on the playground were only the kindergartners and the other first-graders, coasting down the slide and climbing up the fireman's tower. Shocks of grass were pushing up through the gravel, and the first tight honeysuckle buds had appeared along the vine at the back fence. When the recess monitor blew her whistle, the four kids who were on the swings stopped pumping their legs, the two on the low swings skidding to a stop and the two on the high swings making soaring leaps into the gravel. I grabbed hold of the ropes and lifted myself into one of the high swings.

There was nothing I liked better, when I was a girl, than sinking my weight into a swing, feeling the ropes tighten in my hands, and sailing back and forth as high and as fast as I could. As I surged forward, I would stretch myself out as though I were pushing back into a reclining chair, and then, as I dropped back to the ground, I would tuck myself into the narrowest possible ball. It was a continuous fluid motion, almost effortless, and I liked to imagine that I didn't even have to breathe—that all I had to do was open my mouth and the air would flow into me and drain back out with the force of my swinging. I could see the whole playground from the height of the swingset: the boys climbing on the jungle gym, the girls crawling through the tunnel, the row of houses across the street. Kristen Lanzetta was sitting cross-legged on top of the picnic table with Robin Unwer and Andrea Onopa. Oscar Martin was having a gravel war with one of the other boys in our class, hiding behind the fireman's tower so that the recess monitor wouldn't see them. When the whistle shrilled, I let go of the ropes and jumped to the ground.

I landed crookedly, wrenching one of my knees, and I felt a queer tightness in my leg when I began to walk. I hitched over to the picnic table where Kristen was talking with Robin and Andrea.

Their voices fell away, and Andrea looked me up and down. "Why on earth are you walking like that?"

"I don't know. I think I hurt my leg."

"Well, stop it," she said. "You look like a retard."

I hoisted myself gently onto the picnic table, holding my leg rigid so that it wouldn't jar against the corner. "What are you guys doing?" I asked.

"Talking," Andrea said.

"About what?"

"About you. We all think you're a retard. We took a vote."

Kristen cocked her finger and gave Andrea a hard thump on the ridge of her knuckles. A small red mark blossomed there. "Cut it out, Andrea," she said, and she slid over so that I could squeeze into the circle. "We were talking about who we wanted to be our boyfriends. I picked Nathan."

"And I picked William," Andrea said.

"And I picked Oscar," Robin said.

I remembered the dream I had had about Oscar, the one where he kissed me and asked if he could be my boyfriend. Ever since then I had been a different person around him. His seat was right across the aisle from mine, and when we lay with our heads on our desks during Quiet Time I would stare at the back of his neck from behind the covering of my hair, until one day he scribbled a note on a scrap of paper, wadded it into a ball, and popped it across the aisle to me. "Would you knock it off?" it read. My dreams seemed as rich to me as my life (though now I remember very few of them), and I was always a bit surprised when somebody I had dreamed about behaved as though nothing had happened.

A brown oak leaf that had survived the entire winter fluttering on the tip of a branch came pinwheeling down from the tree above the picnic table, landing on one of the benches. I turned to Robin and Kristen and Andrea and said, "I want to pick Oscar, too."

"You can't," said Robin. "I already did."

"That's right," said Kristen. "Robin got first pick, and she picked Oscar. You have to choose somebody else."

"Why can't we both choose Oscar?"

"Because you just can't, that's why." Andrea was massaging saliva into the red mark on the back of her hand, holding it up to her face to look more closely. "Hey, when I rub my hand like this, the skin slides all over the place," she said. "Take a look," and she showed us how the skin pulled and shifted above her bones when she rubbed it.

"Well, if I can't pick Oscar, I don't want to have a boyfriend," I said. "You can play without me."

"I knew you were going to say that," Robin announced. "Didn't I know she was going to say that?" she said.

"You did," Andrea nodded. Then she turned to me and asked, "So why are you always like that?"

"Like what?"

The girls looked at Kristen. She gave a long sigh through her nostrils. I saw her smothering a grin. She said, "You can be kind of bratty sometimes. No offense, Celia, but you can. That's why Robin and Andrea are my best friends now."

Before I could answer, the recess monitor gave three sharp blows of her whistle, and there was a scramble of arms and legs as we ran in a mass from the playground. We lined up along the parking strips to go inside. I tried to signal to Kristen as we passed through the front doors, *Look at me. Hello, I want to tell you something,* but her eyes kept skipping away from me to a place somewhere just past my left shoulder. It was like she could see straight through me.

That afternoon, when I got home from school, I ran immediately up the corkscrew stairs to my bedroom. My dad was calling to me from the kitchen, "Hey, Ceely, what do you think of ravioli for dinner? Celia?" but I didn't answer. I took the porcelain box where I kept my ring collection off the dresser and let it spill out onto the carpet. Then I bent down and sifted roughly through the collection—eighteen different rings and a dozen different colors, all clattering together in my hands.

By the time my dad came to the door, I was lying on my stomach, crying furiously, two or three rings on every finger. "What's wrong, Celia? Come here," he said, "Let me help you," and he lifted me into his arms, sinking back onto my bed. I heard the mattress springs grating as he sat down. "Sshhh, honey, sshhh. It will be all right."

"I—"

I was crying too hard to get the words out.

"I—"

He brushed a strand of wet hair off my cheek and whispered, "That's okay, baby, you don't have to tell me. Let's just sit here for a while." I let myself cry. I rested my forehead on his shoulder and felt the heat soaking through his shirt, a crescent-shaped damp spot that slowly extended into his collar, and I listened as he told me that *everything would be okay*, that *we could have whatever I wanted for dinner, it didn't have to be ravioli, if he'd known I disliked it so much . . .* , that *when he was my age he had a mom and dad who loved him more than anything in this world, and that just like them he would never let anything bad happen to me.*

And the silt spreads, and the water settles, and soon I see myself playing in the backyard, stirring the pond with a crooked stick and climbing onto the stone wall between the maple trees. It was the next day, and the wind was traveling in visible waves though the long grass at the far end of the yard, where the clearing gave way to a thicket of elm trees. I was tightrope-walking along the wall when I noticed Kid standing in the shadow of our deck. He was carrying his baby sister in a sling against his chest.

I called to him, and he came limping over.

"I hurt my leg just like you," I said. "I twisted it jumping off a swing." And then I noticed: "But it's better now." I sat down and let my leg sway back and forth against the wall, tapping at one of the stones with the heel of my shoe.

Kid boosted himself onto the wall and sat beside me. "I was just looking at a spiderweb," he said. "It was empty."

We rested there for a long time without talking. Kid's sister rose and fell against his chest, sometimes with his breath and sometimes with her own. The sun passed behind a cloud. The sky was a deep, hard blue.

Eventually I said, "You're my only friend now."

"I am?" he asked.

"Uh-huh. None of the others like me anymore." I heard a car rolling by on the street. "How come you don't go to school with me?"

"Well, I did go to school for a while," he said, "but then when I got sick my mom and dad started teaching me at home. I guess I just never went back."

"I go every day. Except one time when I pretended I had a fever, and I got to stay home and eat ice cream. Nobody else knows that. Now that you're my best friend, we can tell each other our secrets."

He shrugged. "I'm not sure I have any secrets."

"I bet you do. Like what's your real name? I can never remember."

"I know," he said, and he frowned and shook his head. "I must have told you a thousand times. It's Travis Worley."

"And I never see you anywhere but on this street. Where do you live, anyway?"

He blew at a wisp of his sister's hair so that it stood up in a tiny loop, then smoothed it back down with his palm. He looked me in the eye.

"Would you like to go there?" he asked.

I said that I would.

"Come on, then," he said, and he hopped off the wall. "It's this way."

That was the day when everything changed. I remember that I took his hand, and he led me into the woods, up the rising hill of elm trees, and everything I could see and hear, and everything I could feel on my skin, seemed to melt away and disappear—the leaves, the insects, even the ground beneath my feet. All around me the world was suddenly much clearer and much smaller. I would have been frightened if it were not so beautiful.

For a moment I could still feel the hand of the new kid, whose name I could never remember, or maybe he just never told me, so that I gave up and called him Kid. And then I felt only the tip of his littlest finger. And then that, too was gone. Perhaps when I lost hold of him I went drifting away like a boat whose mooring has snapped, sailing through the currents of the ocean. Perhaps I—

But I do not know.

So much time has passed since then, but even now I remember the life I left behind. I imagine that it is still there waiting for me, and that if only I can see it plainly enough, remember it distinctly enough, I will be able to return to it. I will join my memories together into the wood and frame and hinges of a door, and that door will open, and I will step through it. I see myself racing up the stairs of my house, calling out to the people I knew, to my mom and my dad, Kristen Lanzetta and Oscar Martin, Robin Unwer and Andrea Onopa. They will all be there, milling around my bedroom and wondering where I have been. They will welcome me home with their arms and their voices, help me brush the dirt and the leaves from my clothing, and ask me if I am all right. And I will tell them that I only fell asleep in the elm trees and lost hold of the time. I was their daughter, and I was their friend. I had not meant to keep them waiting so long.

Appearance, Disappearance,
Levitation, Transformation,
and the Divided Woman

First there was the incident at the water park. One of the wooden buttresses supporting the tornado slide collapsed, causing a long section of the tunnel to tilt backward off its axis and crash to the ground. A family of four who had been picnicking underneath were killed instantly, as well as two boys who spilled from a high curve of the chute into the open air. A girl who was inside the tunnel as it gave way, and who must have imagined that a great rush of water was lifting her back to the top, was all but uninjured by the fall, popping safely out onto a cushion of grass. The State Office of Recreational Safety shut the park down that very afternoon, securing the gates with locks the size of human heads. It was just one of those things.

Then, two weeks later, when the paper had relegated news of the event to a quarter column at the back of the local pages, the video arcade burned to the ground. It was an electrical fire, started when a gang of boys knocked a VR machine over into a distribution box. The boys had drilled a hole through a game token and tied it to a line of fishing wire so that they could thread it back out of the machine when they were done playing. When the token got lodged inside, they rocked the machine onto its edge and then tipped it over, running away when its weight carried it through the wall. The room went up in a geyser of sparks. No one was killed in the blaze, though a child who had fallen asleep in the ball crawl suffered second-degree burns on her arms and legs from the heat of the melting plastic.

Finally, only a few days later, the eastern wall of the skating rink was demolished by a wrecking crew who mistook the building for an abandoned warehouse. The warehouse in question was at 1800 Taylor Loop, and the skating rink was at 1800 Taylor Boulevard, and when the manager arrived to unlock the front door, he found a dozen men in hardhats frowning over a pile of concrete at the polished wooden oval of the skating floor.

So it was that Stephanie hired a magician for her son's birthday—though all he had spoken about since the summer began was the party he wanted to have at Wild River Country, and then at Aladdin's Castle, and then at Eight Wheels. When she heard that the skating rink was closed for reconstruction, she had asked him, "What do you think? Wouldn't a magician be fun instead?" and he bent to his comic book with a negligent shrug. "I guess so," he said, and then, after a few seconds, "But he'll probably get hit by a car."

The man she hired wasn't even a very good magician, it turned out, with his ungainly fish hands and his ragged black cape. Brown crumbs littered his mustache from the piece of cake he had eaten when he arrived, and more than once, as Stephanie watched his performance, she saw him pocketing some egg or coin that was supposed to have disappeared into thin air. But the children seemed to enjoy him, and that's what mattered. One or two of them even shouted out in surprise when he released a dove from a silver pan—and they all clapped and laughed when it escaped and perched on his shoulder, pecking at the crumbs in his mustache. All except Micah, that is, who sat staring blankly ahead. Either he was so fascinated by the show that his face had locked in an expression of perfect calm, or he was so bored by it that he was imagining himself at the water park, the wave pool billowing beneath him with the tautness of muscle. Or, Stephanie thought, he was thinking about his father. She couldn't tell.

At the end of his act, the magician said, "And now for my final trick I need a volunteer. Is there anyone in the audience who's *exactly* ten years old?" He glanced uncertainly at Stephanie and mouthed the word "ten," a question, and when she nodded, he continued with his patter. "As I say, a volunteer who's exactly ten years old. Not nine years old and three hundred sixty-four days. Not ten years old and one day. If there's anyone in the audience who's ten years old *on the button,* will that person please come forward? I won't be able to summon the magic without your assistance."

Reluctantly, Micah stood and walked to the magician's side. "You're ten years old?" the magician asked, and Micah nodded. "Hm. That's really something. I would have guessed you were at least twenty-seven."

"Ten," Micah insisted. "On the button."

The trick the magician performed was a simple one: he displayed his hands to the room—they were empty—and then cupped them together and told Micah to strike them with his "two best fingers" while he said the magic words. "And a gold nugget will appear. Are you ready? One, two, three—abracablat!" He opened his hands, and an egg was resting on his palm. The children laughed. "No, that's not it. How does it go? One, two, three—abracablam!" This time it was a plastic novelty whistle. "No, that's not right, either. Ah, yes. One, two, three—abracadabra!" and he removed a lump of pyrite—fool's gold—from his hands. Stephanie wondered for a moment if the man's earlier ineptitude had simply been part of the act, but when he offered the fool's gold to Micah it bobbled off his fingers, made a dinking noise against his belt buckle, and went rolling away.

Micah chased after it. "What do you want me to do with this?" he asked.

"You can keep it, of course. Happy birthday."

"Well, I don't really want it," Micah said. But nevertheless he slipped it into his pocket.

The magician had taken his bow, then mopped the sweat from his forehead with the tail of his cape. It looked as though he planned to gather it around himself and disappear, like a real magician, in a swelling crack of smoke, but instead he let it fall back to his waist, its loose threads clinging to his shirt so that the fabric dimpled and hooked on him. He handed each of the kids a chocolate sucker shaped like a top hat with a rabbit inside it. Then he collected his check from Stephanie, which he had her make out to "Frank Lentini, Magician," and he headed for the front door. Just before he left, Micah took his sleeve and asked him a question: "You're not me coming back from the future to tell me about my life, are you?"

Instead of laughing as Stephanie expected him to, the magician frowned and cocked his head. He seemed for all the world to be thinking about it. "No, son," he finally said. "No, I wish I was. Some tricks even a magician can't perform."

That night, as she was preparing their supper, stirring the ground beef, onions, and chopped green peppers over a flared gas flame, Micah asked her whether his father had called. That was the word he used—the word they both used, always—*father*. He was sitting on a high stool by the telephone, swiveling from side to side on the metal discus of one of the legs as he gripped the kitchen counter. Stephanie's ex-husband had moved to the West Coast shortly after they divorced, taking a promotional job with a movie studio to escape what he called "the change in the weather." This had been his nickname for her from the very first days of their marriage: *the weather. How's the weather today?* he would ask when he woke her up in the morning, running the pads of his fingers over her stomach, or later, when things started to go bad, *Uh-oh, I feel a chill coming on in the weather*, and *I hardly wanted to leave the office today, the weather has been so lousy*, and *Always the same old weather, isn't it?* Then he would drum his knuckles against the nearest hard surface, making the rimshot and cymbal sound that comedians always use to punctuate a joke. Within a year of moving away he had remarried, and within two years he was raising a second son, Jacob, and sometimes Stephanie thought that he had forgotten about Micah altogether. "Your father phoned during the party," she wanted to tell him, "but you guys were having so much fun that we couldn't bear to interrupt you." But the two of them had made a compact: he wouldn't lie to protect his skin if she wouldn't lie to protect his feelings.

"No," she said. "He didn't call. I'm sorry, M."

To which he said, "I want to take magic lessons."

He hoisted himself onto the counter, allowing the stool to spin out from under him and totter across the floor. It shivered in a tight circle like a quarter. Stephanie watched it come to a stop on its legs, still upright.

"Wow," she said. "How on earth did you do that?"

And Micah said, "Magic," and gave a theatrical flicker of his fingers.

The next day Stephanie phoned Frank Lentini, Magician,

and every Tuesday and Thursday afternoon thereafter she delivered Micah to Lentini's studio above the bicycle shop for a ninety-minute lesson. She picked him up at exactly six o'clock, parking by the thin, balding locust tree on the sidewalk and honking twice. He would come out smelling of butane and flash powder, and though she barely noticed the scent when he first sat down in the car, it would intensify as she drove him home, a bitter perfume, until she felt it as a thornlike pinch high in her nostrils. He began to accumulate magic supplies, which he carefully shelved in his bedroom: decks of cards and compressed streamers and even a palm-sized guillotine that could chop a cigarette in two or leave it whole depending on how he manipulated it. "So you're enjoying this, huh?" she asked him one day. "These magic lessons?"

"They're okay. So far none of it's *real* magic, though. Just a bunch of illusions." He shrugged his shoulders. "The Great Lentini says you have to start small."

Stephanie laughed. "You call him the Great Lentini?" She remembered the way he had fumbled with the check she gave him at the birthday party, miscreasing it so that the corners formed jutting triangular wings.

"Uh-huh," said Micah. "I call him the Great Lentini, and he calls me the Great Zakrzewski."

Zakrzewski. This was his father's name, which Micah shared. During the long months of their engagement, after hearing him wearily correct someone's poor pronunciation of it for the thousandth time, Stephanie had decided to keep her own name, the simple Burch. Still, every time she introduced Micah to a new teacher or took him to the doctor's office, she found herself parroting the exact same words: "No, it's not

Zak-ruh-zoo-ski, it's Zuh-krev-ski. No, it's not Zak-ruh-zoo-ski, it's Zuh-krev-ski."

While Micah was taking his magic lessons, she usually went to the park a few blocks away, where she walked beneath the trees, listening to the hissing sound her shoes made as she kicked through the pine needles. That was the summer when it rained every day between four and five o'clock, big drops that left coin-sized impressions when they soaked into the ground, but by the time she stepped outside, all the standing water would have drained or evaporated and nothing would remain but the fresh green smell of leaves in the air. Hundreds of seed-like insects went twitching and flying through the grass, a sight she had always loved, and children ran in packs through the playground. She would sit on a fiberglass bench and watch them.

Though much of her childhood was still a shining path to her, one she could walk down at will, she remembered nothing at all of her life before the age of seven, when she woke in her bedroom from what her parents told her was a high fever. Most people, it was true, did not remember their life before the age of seven, but they were connected to it by a long thread of tastes and associations and family stories, so that they did not notice the loss so readily. In her case, Stephanie felt, that thread had snapped and fallen away in the heat of her fever. She had gone sailing off into her adulthood like a kite. She had a rich life, a bountiful life (I want her to be happy), but when she sat watching the children in the park, running and swinging, shouting and crying, she sometimes wondered about those missing years and whether part of her hadn't gone missing as well, some small shape inside her no bigger than a girl.

When the shadow of the playground structure reached as

far as her bench, she knew that it was time to go, and she would head back to the studio to collect Micah and drive home. She would wait for him to come barreling down the stoop, linen scarves fluttering from the zipper of his backpack. He did not like her to come upstairs to the studio, some hocus-pocus about "breaking the magician's code," and so she rarely did— only the afternoon of his very first lesson and the time she had to pick him up early for a dentist's appointment.

And on one other occasion. It was a muggy evening near the end of the summer, so hot that the line of red ants on the side-walk had all but stopped moving, waiting for the shadow of the locust tree to slant back over their path. Micah had not come out when she honked her horn. She sat through an entire cycle of the traffic light, honked again, and then locked the car and went upstairs. She found him in the anteroom of the studio, kneeling beside Frank Lentini, who was tied to a wooden chair with three long tendons of gray-green rope.

"Hello, Ms. Burch," Mr. Lentini said.

"Hey, Mom." Micah let loose of the knot he was trying to unpick with his teeth. "He was showing me how to escape from a chair, but I tied the ropes too tight."

Stephanie covered her grin with her hand. "I see." She helped Micah free the man, loosening the knots with a hairpin she found in her purse, and after the ropes had fallen away, she told Micah to run and get his backpack.

"Thank you, Ms. Burch," Lentini said, standing and picking the bristles of rope from his shirt.

"You know," she shook her head, "you might be the single worst magician I've ever seen."

The sight of his face wincing and draining of color made her stomach plunge. "Oh, I'm sorry, I—"

"No need to apologize," he said. "I know. It's these damn hands." He held them out like two gloves frozen on a clothesline. "Most mornings it takes me more than one try to even get my shoelaces right."

"Then why on earth did you decide to go into magic?"

"It's always been this way," he sighed. "Everything I really like is just out of my reach. When I was Micah's age, believe it or not, I wanted to perform with an orchestra. But, well . . ." He shrugged and smiled. "Let's just say the world lost a fourth-rate pianist when it gained a third-rate magician. I try to make up for it by being funny. Forgetting people's names, letting the dove eat crumbs out of my mustache, things like that."

"You mean that thing with the dove is part of the act?"

He laughed. "Of course it is. I'm not *that* incompetent."

By this time Micah was standing in the doorway wind-milling his backpack from side to side. "Come *on*, Mom. I'm ready to go. Goodbye, Great Lentini."

"See you next time, Great Zakrzewski. And thanks for setting me free, Ms. Burch. I'll try to repay the favor sometime."

"Likewise," Stephanie answered, realizing only a moment later that what she had said—what both of them had said—had made no sense.

Before they were halfway home she had to stop in the parking lot of a fried chicken restaurant. She told Micah he could run inside and order a to-go box for himself, though she herself waited in the car. For some reason she couldn't stop laughing.

———

That fall, the night of the first hard frost, a water main ruptured in the movie theater, emptying several thousand gallons of water into the lobby. The pipe that burst was behind the snack bar, at the loose socket of one of the elbow joints, and the force of the evacuating water shattered both the candy case and the popcorn bin. When the pool spread into the VR machines, the discharge short-circuited the building's electricity, so that the manager had to open the doors manually the next morning. The water poured outside in a single collapsing wall, he told the newspapers, knocking him off his feet. Cardboard packages of Milk Duds and SweeTARTS surfed past him into the parking lot. "It was like in a cartoon," he said. He closed the theater for remodeling and rewiring and did not reopen it until the new year.

Earlier that same night, a derelict lost half his left arm in an accident at the bowling alley. He had been living in the ball-and-pin retrieval room, it was discovered, sleeping on a blanket behind the machinery and sneaking into the lobby at night to steal hot dogs and pickles from the snack bar. He had been there for weeks, ever since the weather grew cold. Every few days, out of boredom, he would borrow a pin from the belt, drawing a happy face on it with a tube of lipstick before replacing it. No one ever seemed to notice. Late one night, though—a league night—he caught his hand in the rack as the pins shuffled and locked into place. When the apparatus surged forward, it wrenched his arm loose, tearing it off at the elbow. The State Office of Recreational Safety shut the bowling alley down the next day for multiple violations of the occupancy code.

It was three weeks later when a group of college fraternity pledges punched a hole in the ceiling of the Aerospace Museum. They had broken in through the service entrance with a twenty-gallon gas drum, intending to "fly" the Sopwith Camel that was on loan from the Royal Air Force into the gift shop. But they forgot to disconnect the steel cable securing it to the rafters, and when they gunned the engine, the plane made a swinging curve into the ceiling. One of the propeller blades was fractured in the collision, and a strip of canvas was torn from the starboard wing. The boy in the pilot's chair sprained his ankle, but the other pledges were unhurt by the accident. The college placed the fraternity on extended probation.

Stephanie was in her living room, watching a Web report about the event, when the doorbell rang. It was a bleak Sunday afternoon, sheets of rain falling from a mouse-colored sky, and she was wearing three pairs of socks on her feet and a heavy goosedown jacket. She always seemed to be colder the last few weeks of autumn, before the ice and snow began to threaten, than she was in the depths of winter. It was as if the weather became so humiliating after a while that she no longer even felt it. The doorbell rang again and she shouted, "Hold on," muting the volume on the monitor before she answered it.

It was Frank Lentini, dripping wet and holding a capsized umbrella, its metal braces locked inside out in a broomlike cone. "I'm sorry to bother you, but can I come in? I won't take much of your time."

"Of course," Stephanie said. When he stepped inside, the light spread across the sheen of water on his face, sharpening the angles and filling in the planes, so that he looked for a moment like one of the movie stars of her childhood—Ewan McGregor, say, or Hugh Jackman. He squeezed the rain from his hair and let it hang down over his eyes in a dark tangle. Stephanie had to shake her head to clear it of the vision. "You know, you should wear your hair like that all the time. It suits you."

He stared into the middle distance, considering. "I will," he decided. And then: "Listen, is Micah home? I wanted to talk to you two about something."

When she called for Micah, he came pounding down the hall from his bedroom. Lentini asked the two of them to sit on the couch, though he himself remained standing, a pool of water threading off his clothes onto the floor. He told them that he had been asked to participate in the state invitational magic exhibition, which was to be held this year at the Shrine Convention Center. "That's probably why they asked me," he said. "I'm a local practitioner. Anyway, it's a real honor, and I want you to come as my assistant, Micah. That is, if you're up for it. The problem is it's the first weekend of January, and that doesn't give us much time. We'd have to start rehearsing three or four times a week instead of just Tuesday and Thursday. I don't want us—me . . . I don't want me to botch this one up."

"Well, what do you think, M.?" Stephanie asked.

He actually looked excited. "Sounds good to me."

Lentini nodded. "Great, great. So I'll see you tomorrow afternoon? At four-thirty?" He was still carrying his umbrella, and when he looked at the pierced fabric, hanging off the wires like a bat's wings, he frowned. He asked Stephanie, "Do you have someplace I can get rid of this before I go?"

"Are you sure? I thought it went with the hands—a matching set."

He attempted a smile, but it sickened and fell almost immediately. A deep groan rose from somewhere inside him. It sounded like a rockfall echoing through a system of caves.

"I didn't mean that," Stephanie said. "Here, I'll take it," and after he handed it over to her, he showed himself out the door.

The next day, when Micah had finished school, she dropped him off at the studio, and after that he began to meet with Lentini four afternoons a week. He wouldn't tell her anything about the act they were preparing, just that it was going to incorporate "each of the five categories of illusion," and whenever she pressed him, he would say, "You'll have to come see it for yourself. You'll be there, won't you, Mom?"

"I wouldn't miss it," she'd answer, and he would pinch off an impulsive grin, saying, "I know you won't. I see all things. I know all things. I am the Great and Powerful Zakrzewski."

Now and then, half an hour or so before he went to bed, he would show her a simple card trick. He was becoming nimbler and more practiced by the day, and soon, she had no doubt, he would be better than Mr. Lentini. He had taken to rolling a quarter over his knuckles to exercise his fingers, and as she drove him to school in the morning or watched the Web with him at night, she would sometimes catch a glimpse of it out of the corner of her eye, a somersaulting flash of silver, though she could have sworn he was sitting perfectly still. She thought of this diligence, this unexpected skill, as the first feature of his adulthood, rising up in him like a fire climbing a rick of wood, and she found it both fascinating and disturbing. Would she recognize him at all, she wondered, once it had consumed him?

One night, while he was studying for a quiz in long division, his father telephoned for him. Stephanie stood in the kitchen sorting through the expiration dates on the canned goods, trying hard not to listen in as they talked, but she couldn't help but overhear the occasional *yes sir* and *Saturday* and *why not?* After a few minutes, Micah came out of his bedroom and said, "So guess what? He won't be able to make it to the magic show."

"I'm sorry, Micah. Is that why he called?"

"No. I think he called because he's mad at Jacob. They had a fight or something. Jacob called him a liar, so he sent him to his room. But that's okay, he says, because I'm his real son. I've always been the better one." He bit his lower lip, and all at once he was crying.

Stephanie towed him onto her lap, closing her arms around him. "Shhh," she told him. "Shhh."

"How did we get stuck with him, Mom?"

"Oh, sometimes people aren't who you think they are. And sometimes people are exactly who you think they are, but then they go and change on you. It will take you the rest of your life to figure it out, honey."

"But I'm scared of the rest of my life."

"Why?"

"What if I turn out like him?"

"You won't, Micah. You know why? Because you're going to turn out just like me." She kissed the crown of his head. "Either me or Fatty Arbuckle, I'm not sure who yet," and though he did not laugh, she felt him sagging contentedly into her body.

"How did *you* think your life was going to turn out when you were little?" he asked, sniffling.

This was something he liked to try every so often—making a sudden hairpin turn midway through a conversation to ask her about her childhood. He thought that if he did it quickly enough, without warning, he could surprise her into remembering. "I wish I could tell you, M.," she said, and she scratched at the back of his neck, twining her fingers through the wispy commas of short brown hair. "Sorry, kid. Maybe next time."

A few weeks later, not long before the state magic exhibition, Lentini was waiting outside the bicycle shop for her when she delivered Micah for his lesson. He jogged to the curb, rapping playfully on her window, and asked if he could treat the two of them to dinner that night. "In celebration of our act and its finishing touches," he said.

"Sounds good," she told him. "I'll be back at my usual time. Six o'clock," she said, "ravenously hungry."

When she drove to the park, she found it almost deserted. She walked across the cushion of pine needles to the bench by the playground. It was late December, and the wind was blasting so hard that she could hear airborne pieces of gravel pinging against the bars of the jungle gym. The mothers and their children had all gone home for the afternoon, and a small group of teenagers, balancing on the seesaws, was laughing and smoking marijuana cigarettes. She decided to pass the hour in the public library across the street, browsing through the catalogue of books and other printed matter. Then, shortly before six, she collected a dress she had dropped off at the dry cleaner's. When she carried it over the ventilation grille on the sidewalk, the pliofilm bag fluttered and bellied open like a balloon, and she imagined for just a second what it would be like to rise into the air clinging to its hem.

By the time she returned to the studio she was so hungry she could feel it as a swelling tug at the back of her throat.

Lentini was waiting with Micah on the stoop for her, and he drove the two of them to Alouette's, the only French restaurant in town. As soon as they passed through the door, Stephanie caught the mingled scents of bread and coffee and butter, and she heard her stomach complaining audibly. "Are you sure you don't want to check your coat?" Lentini asked as the maître d' showed them to their table.

"No. I'm still freezing."

He shrugged—"It's your sauna"—and guided her by the elbow into her chair. The table was lit by a white candle in a curved silver dish, and Micah began making impressions in the pool of wax around the base, peeling the crust from his skin as it cooled and tossing it back into the flame. After the waiter had taken their orders, Stephanie said, "So, you guys are ready for the big show?"

"We are," Lentini said.

"But you won't tell me what happens?"

"We won't," Micah said. "But—" He turned to Mr. Lentini. "Can I ask her?" and Lentini nodded. "We need a volunteer for the final trick, and we were hoping you would let us pick you."

She asked Lentini, "I don't have to eat crumbs out of your mustache, do I?"

He smiled. "No, nothing like that. I promise we'll take good care of you."

"Okay," she said. "It's settled, then. I'm your volunteer." As the waiter delivered their salads, she allowed her eyes to wander through the restaurant—the polished wooden walls that held a tapered reflection of their bodies; the smoke-blue tiles of the clay floor; the pale stars of the candle flames, swaying in unison whenever the kitchen door opened. "You know, I can't remember the last time I ate in a restaurant like this," she said. And she couldn't. She had been on few dates since her divorce—none at all in the past two years—and they had always ended early in the evening, shortly before her son's bedtime, after a few hours of conversation at a coffeehouse or bar. She subjected each of the men she went out with to a single question, *Could this person be a father to Micah?*, and they were transformed before her eyes, every one of them, into walking repositories of damage.

"That's a shame," Lentini said. His hair was hanging in a tattered line across his forehead, and it looked something like the whisk of oscillating brushes at the automatic carwash. She couldn't help but find the effect comic (as she found everything he did—though why was that?), but she was touched that he had taken her advice. "I try to go someplace nice at least once a month. But, you know, a magician's pay. I can't always manage it."

"Lentini," she said. "That's Italian, isn't it?"

"Sicilian." He drank a sip of water. "I'm named after my great-great-grandfather, Francesco Lentini. He immigrated to the United States when he was just a boy. He was a circus performer—a three-legged man, actually—fairly well known in his day."

Micah looked up from the candle. "No way. You never told me that." He was shaping the soft wax of the brim into crenellations.

"You never asked."

"What did he do when he needed to buy shoes?"

"Well, believe it or not, I know the answer to that. He always bought an extra pair. He would give the fourth shoe, the one he didn't need, to a one-legged friend of his."

"I don't believ—*ow!*" Micah snatched his hand from the candle. "Ow. Dang it. I burned myself." He plugged his ring finger into his mouth, then pulled it loose and showed it to Stephanie. It had a tiny red mark the size and shape of a wood spider on it. Lentini dipped a corner of his napkin into his water glass, righting it just before it toppled. He pressed the napkin to the burn, and Micah surrendered a groan. "I'll still be able to perform on Saturday, won't I?" he asked.

Lentini gave his shoulder a gentle squeeze. "Don't worry. It's not your thumb, and it's not your index finger, so there's no real loss of dexterity. You should be fine."

Stephanie found a Band-Aid in her purse. "Here you go, honey," she said, and after Micah had taped it around his finger, she asked, "So you're *really* not going to tell me what I've volunteered for?"

"We're really not," said Micah. "It would spoil the surprise. I can only tell you—" But before he could finish, the waiter arrived with their meals, and he lapsed into a grinning silence.

Stephanie had ordered the escargot, Lentini the salmon filet, and Micah the inevitable hamburger from the children's menu. As she smoothed the napkin over her lap and reached for her plate, Micah took hold of her wrist. He shook his head, then leaned in as if to confide a secret. "What is it, M.? Ready to tell me?" she asked.

"You know those are snails, don't you?" he said.

Later, when she was finally home from the magic show, the cut on her neck bandaged and the soot washed from her face, she would read about the fire in the newspaper. A trio of Central

American acrobats had been invited to perform as the exhibition's final act, and they were assembling their props behind the curtain when an arc light burst overhead. A spark, or perhaps a fragment of hot glass, touched the ring of flash paper they had prepared, igniting it. The fire ought to have died away then and there, but the safety curtain had been removed for cleaning, replaced with a curtain of untreated cotton, which collected the flame and carried it into the rafters. Live cinders and feathers of ash began raining down over the audience, and within minutes the entire auditorium was ablaze, the air weaving and swaying in the heat. The fire inspector attributed the conflagration to "the careless employment of flammables," and the State Office of Recreational Safety promised to lobby the legislature for the prohibition of flash paper, "the inventor of which," the newspaper reported, "himself died in such a discharge while drying sheets of the material in his cellar." Two people were killed and dozens more injured in the blaze. The wooden joists of the Shrine Convention Center rose above the ashes like a blackened rib cage.

But on Saturday afternoon, as she changed into her blouse and skirt, Stephanie was anticipating the show with the same blend of fear and nervous excitement as Micah. She had watched the signs of his restlessness all week, absorbing scraps and pieces of it into herself. He spent the better part of Saturday morning tossing a rubber ball onto the roof while she dusted the recesses of her keyboard with a Q-tip and then cleaned between the tines of her comb with a straight pin and then organized the books on her bookshelf according to the color spectrum. As he muttered to himself in his bedroom, rehearsing the act one last time, she found herself pacing between the stove and the refrigerator, singing a song about a giraffe that she must have learned in Micah's nursery school days.

A few minutes before they left, she came out snapping a loose thread from her skirt and discovered Micah waiting for her in the living room, paging through a magazine in his magician's outfit, a tuxedo with tails and a long black cape. He looked up at her. "You're not going to wear that, are you?"

"I was planning to, Micah."

He shook his head. "No, no, no," he insisted. "Wear pants," and so she went back to the closet and changed into a pair of khakis.

It had been raining lightly, intermittently, for most of the afternoon, and as she drove to the Shrine Convention Center she watched the drops stippling the pavement, a network of shifting white splashes that resembled a swarm of gnats flickering around each other in the sunlight. She found it hard to keep a watch on the traffic. It was as though her center of awareness had traveled in a split line from her brain to her eyes. She would be the perfect audience today, she thought, the ideal mark, easily distracted by flashes of color and light.

She let Micah out beneath the covered drive and then parked the car and walked back inside, carrying the two umbrellas she had brought, one hooked over each arm. The rain was at a lull, with only the barest scattering of drops blowing from the trees, and she did not need to cover herself.

Lentini was squatting precariously in the foyer, straightening Micah's bow tie. He braced himself every few seconds with his palm. When he noticed her, she said, "This is for you," and handed him the extra umbrella. It was a mahogany cane umbrella with a thick plaid canopy, and she had knotted a ribbon around the handle. "It's a good luck umbrella. Guaranteed to last you through even the worst weather."

He stumbled to his feet, his cape brushing grit from the floorboards. "It's the perfect present," he said, his eyes shining with a sidelong light. "And I mean that. Thank you." He took her hand. "But we have to go backstage now."

"Okay. I'll be ready for my moment in the spotlight."

"We'll look for you in the audience." And he bowed to her, prompting Micah to do the same.

After they had left, Stephanie took the back door into the auditorium and selected a seat along the center aisle, two-thirds of the way from the front. The chairs were made of an old, yellowing wood with strips of lacquer curling from the armrests like pencil shavings, and she could feel the bristles scratching against her skin whenever she shifted her posture. Someone had pulled a strand of carpet loose at her feet, and it stretched halfway across the aisle, a zigzagging brown ligament with hanks of white matting at the twists. The other chairs filled slowly around her. Just before the lights dimmed, she felt a rough hand grasping her upper arm and heard a voice say, "Ruth." She turned to look.

It was the man sitting behind her, his arm extending through the gap between the seats. "Oh my God. I'm sorry." His face lost its color, and he retrieved his hand. "It's just . . . from this angle . . . I thought you were someone else. Please excuse me," he said, and he hid his face behind his program.

This sort of thing happened to her all the time—more often, she suspected, than it did to most people. She would be waiting in line at a restaurant or testing the tomatoes at the grocery store when someone would stop short and call her by the wrong name, mistaking her for some old friend or cousin or ex-lover. Once, on a trip she took to New York City, an older man had caught hold of her sleeve in the lobby of a hotel and asked her if she was somebody named Sheila, or Sally. Even when she told him she wasn't, his gaze remained peculiarly insistent. He repeated the name a few times (was it Sheila or Sally?), striking hard at it, like a hammer rapping a nail, and when he reached for her cheek she had fled to the elevator. She had seen him walking toward her as the doors closed. There was a haunted look about him, as though he couldn't quite decide if she was real. This was years ago, on her last vacation with Micah's father, and when she told him about the incident, he had laughed as though it was the funniest thing he had ever heard. She had not been back to New York since.

She could hear the conversations around her dwindling to whispers as the auditorium fell dark and an overlapping chain of spotlights blazed onto the stage. There were more than thirty performers in the exhibition, and every time one of them finished his act a crackling of applause would fill the air, thousands of palms meeting and parting in delight or polite obligation. Every single seat in the room was taken, and when Stephanie swiveled around to look up the aisle, she saw a clutch of bodies standing against the back wall. Where had all these people come from, she wondered. She saw conferences advertised almost every weekend on the marquees of the local hotels—PINEWOOD LODGE WELCOMES THE REGIONAL SCRABBLE-PLAYERS CONVENTION . . . GREETINGS FROM BUDGET INN TO THE RETIRED AUTOWORKERS ASSOCIATION—but she had always imagined them as just a few tired bodies gathered around a card table or a cheese tray. Were they always this crowded?

Late in the second act, the curtain drew shakily closed and the emcee announced, "Now, before our final performers, the Acróbatas Puntarenas, we have one last act. Please welcome local magician Frank Lentini and his assistant Micah." At that, Lentini wheeled a long, shallow cabinet onto the apron, and Micah followed behind him carrying a pedestal. Most of the earlier performers had been true professionals, more than merely capable—there was the man whose clothing changed color each time he turned his back to the audience, and the woman who made her three large collies disappear through a pair of hoops—and Stephanie was worried that Lentini and Micah would embarrass themselves. The only blunders they made, though, were so ridiculous that she was sure they were deliberate.

First Lentini covered the pedestal with a scarf and called upon "the dove, symbol of purity" to appear, but when he whisked the scarf away a pigeon was strutting around there, preening in the white disk of the spotlight. "Marlboro!" Lentini scolded. "How did you get here?" Lentini wandered to the other side of the stage, where he told the audience, "We call him Marlboro because he's always looking for another light, folks. Micah, will you do the honors?" The pigeon pivoted its head around, nibbling sourly at a ruff of feathers, and Micah draped the scarf back over it. When he pulled it away, the pedestal was empty. Then he said, "Rise," and tapped the pedestal three times with his wand. To Stephanie's fascination, it gave three lunging hops across the stage, hovering in midair for a second each time before it landed. Though she looked carefully, she could not see the glint of wires around it, their finely drawn slant through the dust and the light, and she wondered if Lentini had concealed some sort of motor-and-spring arrangement inside it.

When the pedestal had arrived at his feet, he said, "Now let's see if we can convince our friend the dove to join us," and he placed his top hat on the stand and struck it with his wand, then reached inside and pulled out an upright cane umbrella, the same one she had given him earlier. "That's strange," he said, scratching at his scalp. "I could have sworn I put that dove in there." He batted his hand around inside the hat and found nothing, but when he opened the umbrella, absentmindedly twirling it over his head, the dove dropped out onto his shoulder. The audience laughed.

Every so often the curtain behind him would give a weak ripple and then bulge forward suddenly—it reminded Stephanie of nothing so much as a swamp releasing bubbles of methane—and she was watching for it to happen again when she heard Lentini saying, "And now for our final illusion, we need a volunteer," and before she knew it, she was standing next to him on the stage.

"What's your name, ma'am?" he asked.

"Stephanie. Stephanie Burch."

"Okay, Stephanie Burch. Are you ready to see what it's like when one part of you is over here and the other part is *waaay* over there?" he said, pointing across the stage, and then he put his hand to a long, shallow cabinet, patting its side. "Are you ready, that is, to see yourself cut in two?"

Oh, Lord, she thought, and she had a fleeting vision of herself spilling great cataracts of blood from her waist. But she said, "I guess so," and Lentini led her to a stool at the head of the cabinet.

Micah was waiting to hold the top half of the lid open for her. "Curl your knees to your chest," he whispered as he escorted her inside. "You'll be okay. We've got another lady in there."

She felt her feet pressing up against a ledge as she slid inside, and a pair of hands took her ankles from below, securing them safely behind it. She was surprised by how much space there was around her, a sort of hidden basin that curved around her back, deep enough for her to sink into quite comfortably. When she stuck her head out the end of the cabinet, she saw Lentini hovering over her. The glare from the footlights bleached the tips of his mustache into a glistening white trail. She could have sworn she heard the sound of breaking glass, and then a sizzling rush of air, but when nobody else seemed to notice, she decided she must have been mistaken.

"Ladies and gentlemen," Lentini said, "We have secured the locks. I will now attempt to slice Ms. Burch in two," and he winked at her. A quick second later she heard the *shnikt* of the blade entering the cabinet, and she gasped. Her toes twitched involuntarily—which meant that they were still there—and she felt a hard pulse of heat against her face. When Lentini wheeled her around, she caught a glimpse of two feet projecting from the other half of the cabinet, churning around like paddles, and then she looked at the ceiling. She must have been the first person to see the flames crawling along the timbers, a dozen blazing lines reaching all the way from the flies to the gallery. It was not until a long petal of burning wood floated down, throwing off yellow sparks, that the first shout arose from the audience.

Afterward, everything happened so quickly. The sixty-year-old oak of the rafters began to blacken and crumble, sending chunks of cinder into the aisles, and the seats with their peeling lacquer went up like tinder. Her head was facing toward the curtain, which was a wavering sheet of flame, but it was not difficult to hear the tumult in the audience. The outcries of people singed by falling embers. Their footfalls as they ran toward the exits. The explosive crack of one of the doors being wrenched off its hinges. She pushed at the lid of the cabinet, but it would not open, and when she called for Micah, he did not answer.

Then she heard him saying, "We need to unlock them. They're stuck in there," and Lentini shouted, "There's no time. We'll have to roll them outside ourselves."

She shut her eyes against a bright flaring of the curtain, and when she looked again, Lentini was standing over her, gripping the cabinet in his large white hands. "We're taking you out the side door," he said. "Hang on. You'll be okay."

Before she could react, she felt herself bumping down a row of stairs, her neck razing against the edge of the cabinet's window with each jolt. A laceration opened beneath her left ear, and she tried to bring her hand to it, but she couldn't reach that far. She felt like a patient strapped to a gurney. She remembered walking along a fragment of stone wall. She was staring straight into Lentini's face, which was grimacing with the effort of steering her through the crowd, and beyond him into the fire and the pall of smoke. The entire scene kept jerking to the left and right as people butted against Lentini or the cabinet in their rush for the door. One of the birds flapped into the loft of the auditorium, its wings taking flame as it tried to push its way through, but she could not tell whether it was the dove or the pigeon. An elbow plunged into her frame of vision, and then a metal crossbar, and then she was outside.

The air was cold, and she could see tree limbs and telephone wires joining and separating in the sky above her. There was a clatter of wheels as she was jostled over the curb onto the asphalt, and still Lentini kept trolleying her away from the building. When she looked to the right, she saw the other half of the cabinet rolling alongside her. Micah was gripping the railing, a black streak of char on his face, and two small feet were sticking out the other end. One of them was missing a shoe. She wondered who the woman inside was.

Once they had passed the last row of cars, Lentini drew to a stop and doubled over, taking in several deep drafts of air. "Okay," he said when he had finally caught his breath, "let's put you two together"—he gasped again—"and get you out of there."

He brushed a fleck of ash from her cheek, blowing it away like an eyelash, and to her surprise she felt a shiver travel across her shoulders and down her back. Her toes curled, pressing against the ledge inside the cabinet. It was a sensation she recognized from her first high school dances, when she was fourteen years old and her date would fan his fingers across her hips, moving out of time with the music to sway up against her. Though her body was aching and bruised, she felt herself smiling.

The sky had cleared and the sun had fallen, and as Lentini wheeled her into position, she saw clusters of sparks climbing into the stars. They faded to a dull orange just before they disappeared, but for a few seconds they seemed to alter the shape of the constellations—wrapping a hunter's snare around the Pleiades, returning Andromeda to Cassiopeia. It was a map of a different sky, one that wandered and changed before her eyes, a sky where all the old mythologies came back to life and the stories were never about what she thought they were about.

The Telephone

I was sleeping soundly when the telephone rang. It was three or four in the morning, no later, and though my eyes flicked open on strings, it took me a few moments to waken completely into my body. I stared at Janet, who was frowning in her sleep. The digital clock was glowing behind her shoulder, but all I could see of it were two blue spears radiating toward the ceiling. It looked like the moon must look rising out of the ocean.

The phone rang again, and then again. A floating sound. A strange, loose rattling.

This would be hell, I thought.

It was a question I asked myself all the time: What would the world be like if this moment lasted forever—if God took it in His hands and stretched it out over eternity? I experienced a dozen little heavens and hells every day. I waited for the answering machine to catch and roll its announcement. When it didn't, I picked up the telephone. The dial tone gave its usual blended shrill, and I put the phone back in its cradle. But I could still hear the ringing coming from some other room. Who could be calling so late, I wondered.

I got out of bed and checked the second phone in the kitchen, the cell phone in Janet's purse, even the front door, in case the doorbell was malfunctioning. Nothing. Every ring seemed to be coming from a different place, as though the entire house had buckled together like a piece of fabric, making the signal warp and bend. Finally, listening carefully, I followed the sound upstairs, tracing it down the hall into Celia's bedroom. I opened the door, ready to leap at the first ring, and when it came I knelt on the carpet, opening Celia's toy chest.

It was her Walt Disney Talk-to-Me Telephone, the kind with likenesses of all the Disney characters on the buttons. It wasn't a real phone, just a toy, but when you pressed the right sequence of buttons—seven in a row—the bell would jingle and one of the characters would speak to you. Mickey Mouse, Goofy, Uncle Scrooge. We had given it to Celia on her seventh birthday, and it had lain inside her toy chest ever since. I disentangled the cord from a bag of jacks and the top half of a Barbie doll, and then from a flexible rubber horse that had become braided between the loops, and set the phone on Celia's bed. Her sheets and comforter were flawlessly smooth, like the surface of a puddle. Four years ago she had gone missing—four years, five months, and twenty-five days—and the impression of her body had long since risen from the mattress. It had been only a few weeks since we finally held the memorial service for her.

The phone rang again, and I answered it. "Hello?"

"Hello? Dad? Is that you?"

I recognized the voice immediately. It was Celia's.

"Dad? Dad? Can you hear me?"

The telephone receiver was made of a soft hollow plastic that felt almost weightless in my hand, far too light to carry the sound of her voice. "I can hear you," I said. "There's some interference, though."

"Thank God. I've been trying to reach you for . . . it seems like forever. I thought maybe you weren't there anymore."

I bowed my head, tracing my fingers over the long smooth prow of Jiminy Cricket's face. "Of course I'm here."

"I know that now."

"I wouldn't dream of leaving this place, not without knowing you were safe."

A sharp fluttering of static bloomed over the line, and I missed the first part of what she said.

"—all the time. You and Mom both. I always wondered who would answer, though."

"You sound so much older," I said. I felt a knuckle of tears expanding inside my throat.

"Well, I am, I guess. It's been—what? Twenty years?"

"It's been four. Since March 1997." I was sitting delicately on the very rim of her bed so that I wouldn't rumple the covers. I could almost picture her sleeping there. She would look just like she used to—with her hands, balled into fists, stowed inside her pillowcase. "The last time I saw you, you wouldn't quit singing. It was driving me crazy."

"I remember." Amazing how you can hear a person smiling. "*When the sky's in your eye, and the pizza's too high, that's for-sure-ay*. It feels more like twenty to me."

"I'm sorry, Celia. I should have been watching. If I hadn't sent you outside . . ."

I thought she was going to tell me it wasn't my fault, or that I couldn't have done anything to change it, the same thing that everybody else had been telling me for the last four years, but instead she said only, "Thanks," and then coughed once, quietly.

"You blame me, don't you? You don't know how many times I've wished I had that morning to do over again. You have to believe me."

"Dad, I can't talk much longer. Other people are waiting here."

"Hold on," I said. "Don't go yet. Just tell me where you are."

"I'm back," she answered.

There was a strangled series of ticks, and the line went dead. No dial tone, just a deep, impassive silence. I pushed the disconnect button a few times, but nothing happened. Then, as an experiment, I dialed a seven-digit number. The phone produced the gravelly quack of Donald Duck, "Oh boy, oh boy, will you go swimming with me?" I hung up. My ear felt bruised and numb, and I realized that I had been pressing against it with the receiver, bearing down hard.

I had heard somewhere there are two things you cannot do in a dream: you cannot read letters and numbers, and you cannot control the gradation of the light. I looked at the stack of books on Celia's dresser. *Matilda. Amy's Eyes. The Saggy, Baggy Elephant.* When I flipped the light switch by her door, the bulb overhead shone with a dazzling white light, hanging from the ceiling like an apple from a bower. I could smell dust burning away from the glass. When I shut it off, the room went dark again.

It was still night outside, and I stood watching a tiny gray moth that had fastened itself to the window screen separating its wings every few minutes in the breeze. An hour later a bird began to call, a single plunging note that it repeated after ten seconds, and then after another ten, and then, when it received no answering call, fell quiet. An hour later the paper boy bicycled past, slinging the newspaper onto my lawn inside a plastic yellow sleeve.

Then it was morning.

Janet was already showering by the time I returned to the bedroom, currents of steam spilling from the open door. Our house was an old one, with poor ventilation, and she saw no reason to lock herself into the bathroom every morning. "All it does is fog up the mirror," she said. "I can't see a thing when I turn off the water. I can barely even find the towel. Besides, it's only the two of us, Christopher, at least for now. And we're old hat, baby. You can dangle as much as you want to as far as I'm concerned."

"No need to explain yourself," I said. "I love the way you dangle."

But I couldn't shake the habit of shutting the door in case Celia came wandering through.

I was making the bed when I saw the light on the answering machine flashing, which was odd, since I couldn't remember hearing the phone ring again. I touched the play button and listened to the message. "Hey, Janet. It's Kimson. I'm at the station and it's late, but I wanted to hear your voice. This is your voice mail, isn't it? I hope I called the right number. Is this the right number? Anyway, let me know when I'll be able to see you again." He paused a few seconds as a chain of footsteps tapped past him. "Okay, they're gone. I think that's all I had to say. Call me, Janet. I'll be waiting. Bye."

There is a certain tone of voice that new lovers, who are just beginning to discover each other's bodies, always use to speak to each other: a proud, patient hunger—proud, in fact, because it is patient. Even when they try to disguise it, you can hear it in the way they say each other's names, as if they have changed suddenly from abstract nouns to concrete ones, from something you merely think about to something you can take in your hands. The sound tings out like a crystal bell.

I erased the message on the answering machine and watched the tape respool.

I was lathering my face at the mirror when Janet climbed out of the shower, stepping into a bath towel which she wrapped twice around her body and bound in a twist over her breasts. She stood beside me brushing her hair out. "Kimson called," I said.

She did not stop brushing, but the rhythm of her stroke shortened. "About Celia?"

"He didn't say. He wants you to call him back." I scraped the first width of shaving cream from my cheek and a band of red-stippled skin appeared. "Something about working late last night. I can call him myself if you want me to."

"No, that's okay. I had a question I needed to ask him anyway."

I could hear the embarrassment in her voice, and when she lowered her head, whipping her hair forward so that she could brush it against the grain, I saw the root of her neck coloring. The truth was that I had been aware of the affair for some time, from the days when it was no more than a gaze and a softened handshake, and she must have realized this. We were long past being able to conceal ourselves from each other.

Kimson was the head of the local police force, which had been searching for Celia ever since the afternoon she went missing, and Janet had spoken to him almost every day since then, visiting the station to see how the investigation was progressing. He tried to be reassuring—I knew that—but what can you do when there's nothing to go on, when a person just vanishes, lifted like a spirit from her own backyard? I myself could offer very little. Sometimes Janet came home in the evening and found me still wearing my boxer shorts, standing as lifeless as a statue at the window that looked out on the stone wall between the maple trees, the spot where I had last seen Celia playing. "How was your day?" she would ask, and when I didn't answer she would continue: "You didn't have one, you say? Well, that's interesting, Christopher. What's that? How was mine, you wonder? Mine was . . . hard. Mine was very hard, thanks for asking." Once, not long ago, she was telling me about a movie she had seen, *A.I.*, which she described as "a living wreck." Then she looked me up and down and said, "You would probably like it," and we both laughed, because it was true. Kimson had his strength to give her, and his vigor, and his desire, and I had only the memory of our life before it changed. Strength and desire always outshine memory. I found it hard to summon up much resentment.

When Janet had finished with the brush, she pulled a honey-combed tangle of hair from the bristles and let it fall into the trash. "Do you need to get into the shower? Want me to vamoose?" Sometimes she would use words like this—*vamoose, yonder, debacle*—just because she thought they were funny. But there was a flatness to her voice this morning, an age-old weariness that I could only hear as contrition.

"Of course I don't want you to vamoose," I said. "Take all the time you need."

She met my eyes in the mirror. "I think I had better

vamoose." She set her brush on the counter, squaring it against the edge of the sink with a deliberate click. Then she pressed her palm quickly to my back. Half a second later she was gone. I shut the door.

It was not until I had showered, dressed, and eaten breakfast that I realized I had forgotten to tell her about Celia and the phone call, and by then she had already driven into town.

In addition to playing clarinet in the Community Orchestra for which Kimson played contrabassoon, Janet also worked part-time as its publicity director—a paid position—booking performance spaces, pinning fliers to church bulletin boards, buying radio ads on the local classical station, and sending concert circulars to season-ticket holders. She set her own hours, depending on when the next performance date was and how much interest each particular program generated, but she almost always worked from late morning to late afternoon three or four times a week. When she had finished for the day, she would go for a walk along the reservoir, or head to the police station to ask about Celia, or take in a midday movie. Sometimes she would drive for hours through the tree preserves to the south of town, beads of transparent sap collecting on her windshield. I knew that I could not expect to see her home before five o'clock.

I heard a school bus applying its brakes on the street, its heavy, blocklike body rocking and scraping to a halt. It was the elementary school bus—the middle and high school buses came half an hour later—and it always stopped at the end of my front walk. I cracked the door open to watch the children climb inside.

One morning (an entire week of mornings, in fact) I had sat on the front porch with a mug of coffee in my hand to observe the whole procedure: the children congregating in knots and twosomes on my lawn, pulling video games and Matchbox cars from their backpacks, prying up wedges of sod with their shoes. Some of them had been Celia's classmates, and seeing them filled me with a wonderful, open-pored sadness, as though I could understand the whole world if I only looked carefully enough. They seemed both much older and much younger than she was—much older and much younger than she would ever be. She had been seven for so long by then that by the time she was ten or eleven, I thought, she would be ageless. At the end of that week, one of the boys snapped a rubber band at the front of my house, letting fly with it just before he stepped onto the bus. It sailed over the grass and landed at my feet. Since then, I had made it a point to watch the children only from behind the front door. I didn't want to become someone I wasn't: that-man-who's-always-staring-at-us.

When the bus pulled away, I walked out onto the porch and took a few deep breaths. A wind chime threw its shadow onto my face, its struts and vanes rotating slowly in the September air. A dog barked from behind a nearby fence. I collected the newspaper and went back inside.

I passed the day reading the newspaper and a J. G. Ballard novel and writing long, dissociated sentences in my notebook. I was writing sentences again—I had come at least that far—but I could never seem to turn them into stories, into living worlds. I cooked lunch and then dinner for myself and swept a few crisp leaves from the back deck, and when the sun fell I sat in the stairwell watching the house fill with a scorched orange light. It was seven o'clock and Janet still was not home. I tried calling her cell phone number, but when I dialed, I found her phone chirping on the living room sofa, where I had left it the night before. I couldn't help but remember how it had felt the afternoon that Celia disappeared, when I realized I did not know where she was.

That diving-bell sensation in my stomach. The terrible flash of guilt.

I had to restrain myself from calling the police station to report Janet missing.

Shortly before midnight the telephone rang, and I rushed to the kitchen to answer it. "Hello? Janet?" There was no one on the line. When I heard a second ring, I ran immediately to Celia's bedroom and knelt on the floor beside her Walt Disney Talk-to-Me Telephone, which was still resting placidly on her toy chest.

I put the receiver to my ear. "Is that you? I'm here, Celia," I said.

"I'm here, too," she replied. And I sank my forehead onto the worn rope handle of her toy chest.

"Thank God." My heart beat in my ears with the slow pounding sound that waves make underwater. "I didn't know whether I would ever hear from you again."

"Well, I wasn't sure I would be able to call back so soon, but I found another telephone. Listen, Dad, is Mom there? I was hoping to talk to Mom this time." Her voice was clearer than it had been the night before, and I imagined for a second that she was on her way home, traveling toward me in a fast car, its wheels carrying her steadily closer.

"Your mom is . . . out for a while. She didn't say where she was going"

"Oh. Okay. Will you tell her I wanted to talk to her, then? Tell her I said that I miss her."

"Of course. I meant to let her know about our conversation this morning, but—" I interrupted myself. "Celia! You have to tell me where you are! We've been searching for you all this time, but we haven't been able to find you. I guess you know that. But we've tried everything, Celia. Everything. If you tell me where you are, I can call the police and have somebody pick you up."

"I'm not really sure where I am. That's the problem. Everything is still kind of blurry."

It occurred to me that she might not be alone. "Are you okay? Are you in danger?"

"I'm fine, Dad."

"Is somebody listening in, then? If somebody else is there, just tell me—tell me you feel hungry. Or tell me you need to wash your hands."

A threadlike laugh passed through her voice. "There are people all around, Dad. But I don't think any of them are paying attention to us."

"You can talk, then?"

"I can talk, but I don't know for how long. I used my last quarter, so we'll probably get cut off pretty soon. Anyway, there's something I need to tell you. About what happened. I was—" The sentence was broken in two by a pocket of silence,

and when Celia's voice returned, she said, "That was the opera-
tor, Dad. I was right. I'm out of time."

"Can you give me the number there?" I asked. "I'll call you
right back."

"Okay, hold on a second." I heard her mumbling something
to herself. "Well, the first two numbers are scratched out, but
the rest of it is two-five-seven—"

The line disengaged with a muffled pop. In frustration I
jabbed at the keypad with my palm, and a hiccuping chuckle
came through the receiver: "Ah-*hyuk*. This is Goofy. Can I come
over and play?" I put the phone back in its cradle.

I stood and gazed out the arched window above the toy
chest, just as I had the night before. Its glass carried a reflection
of the light from the hallway, a tiny split yellow moon, and I
had to shield the glare from my eyes to see outside. A car was
parked at the curb. When I looked into the front seat, I saw
Janet sitting peacefully next to Kimson, her head resting in the
crook of his arm, his hand inscribing circles in her hair.

Early the next morning I woke to hear Janet talking in the
kitchen. She was using the sort of impassioned whisper that
slices through the air like a dart or a bullet, as loud as any rally-
ing cry, though I was certain she thought I could not hear her.
We had not spoken the night before. She had come inside after
half an hour, tiptoeing up the stairs, and I had pretended to be
asleep, listening to her as she brushed her teeth and cleaned her
face and put on the billowing white T-shirt she liked to wear to
bed. When she lay down beside me I curled narrowly around
my stomach, imagining what it would be like to say, "Janet, we

need to talk about this," or, "Janet, it's time we came clean," until I faded imperceptibly into my dreams and then opened my eyes to a gleaming blue sky.

I could hear her in conversation with someone. "No, Kimson. No, we talked about this last night," and I pressed the mute button on the bedside phone to listen in. "Look, you've been fine with leaving the decisions up to me so far," Janet said. "And we agreed right at the beginning that that's how it would be—everything is my call. So why is that a problem all of a sudden?"

"Because I'm good for you," Kimson answered. "And you're good for me. And you know that, but you won't admit it."

"I *do* admit it," she said.

"There." He gave a sandpapery laugh. "Then we're agreed."

"We're agreed, but so what? I need to give Christopher another chance. That's all there is to it. I have to see where my marriage is heading."

"I know. Your marriage." He paused. "Janet, I've been watching your marriage for four years, just about as closely as you have. Christopher isn't going to get any better. He just isn't."

"See, but you can't say that. It's too soon to tell."

"Of course I can tell. The way he floats around inside that house—"

I slipped the phone back into its mounting, folded the sheets down, and climbed out of bed.

Some thirty minutes later, when I had showered and dressed, I met Janet in the kitchen. She was loading a coffee mug and an egg-stained plate into the dishwasher, and the cuff of one of her sleeves was darkened with a half-circle of tap water. "Morning," she said, and I repeated the word: "Morning." Without comment I watched her wring her sleeve into the sink and pad from the kitchen in her slippers, settling onto the living room sofa, where she turned on the television. I poured a packet of maple and brown sugar oatmeal into a bowl and brought the pot of lukewarm water on the stove to a fresh boil. When it was hot enough, I stirred the water into the oatmeal and waited a few seconds for it to cool, watching the surface pock and dimple as some of it evaporated into steam.

I could hear a news report being broadcast in the other room, that imposing ceremonial baritone. "Sweet Christ," Janet said, and she boosted the volume. "Christopher, come here, you need to see this."

What if the dead and the missing can communicate with us through the objects they have left behind? Blankets and dresses and favorite sweaters. Passport photos and stacks of novels. Glasses and wristwatches and rings. I have seen men whose wives have died pressing lockets and combs to their lips as though they could feel them breathing, women who have lost their husbands holding frayed shirts and jackets to their ears as though they could hear them speaking. And I have noticed that whenever a child vanishes her friends and neighbors will assemble shrines to her memory, decorating her school locker or the chain-link fence behind her house with all the things that were most familiar to her—teddy bears and soccer trophies and snapshots of her family. We leave our parents and marry and follow jobs to other cities, carrying everything we own from one place to another, arranging it all around us, and I have heard people whose houses have burned to the ground say that when the fire took their belongings, the lives they knew turned to ash along with them, abandoned to the flames with their books and clothing and furniture. No one can doubt that we are more than the possessions we keep. Still, it is true that rooms take on the character of the people who live in them, and objects the features of the people who use them. Is it too much to imagine that when the world wrenches fiercely to one side, bearing us away by violence or chance or some fleeting compulsion of the landscape, we cling to the objects we loved the most?

Two days later, when Celia called again, I recognized the jingling of her telephone almost immediately—a high-pitched wobbly tone, muffled in plastic. I hurried upstairs and answered it just as it began to ring again, clipping it off at the first ting of the bell. It was Thursday afternoon, and Janet was at the Community Orchestra office, sending out postcards to announce the postponement of the Saturday-night Mendelssohn concert. I held the phone to my ear. "Hello? Celia?"

"It's me, Dad," she said. "We got cut off."

"I know. Are you okay? Can you talk?"

"Uh-huh. I brought some extra quarters this time."

"Good." Again, I felt a knot forming in my throat. "I'm relieved you're still there." I leaned my hand against the window, which had been warmed by the sunlight, and the glass shifted in its frame with a small popping noise. A grasshopper resting on the ledge outside sprang away, motoring its wings. "I've been so worried about you," I said.

"You don't need to be. I'm better now."

"You're better now? . . . Celia, what happened that day? I need to ask."

"Oh, Dad, Dad." She turned the words into a little tune. "It was so long ago that I only half remember. But if you want me to try, I will."

"Try," I said to her.

"Okay," she said. "Okay, I promise I'll try. Do you know what it feels like when you're drifting off to sleep and all of a sudden something yanks you awake? Well, think of that in reverse—that's what it was like. I was playing outside, and I felt this tingle in my body like something was going to happen, and then it did. Something jerked me right off the wall. It felt like a giant arm. Then everything was dark, and I didn't know how much time had passed, and I wasn't sure where I was at first. I had trouble moving my arms and legs, but I heard some sort of jingling noise when I shifted my head. It sounded like coat-hangers knocking together. I was so tired and dizzy that it took me a long time to figure anything out. Eventually, somebody gave me some water."

"Who?" I asked. "Who was it?"

"I don't know. I couldn't see very well because there was something covering my eyes, but I did hear them moving around. There was more than one of them, I think. I never saw their faces, but I'm pretty sure that's true. Anyway I must have passed out after they fed me. By the time I woke up they had taken me someplace else. It was no place I'd ever been before. I never did find out exactly where it was. I know how I got out, and I *thought* I knew how long I was there, but I never knew that."

When I sighed into the mouthpiece I heard the sound cycling through the receiver, channeled and exaggerated so that it sounded like a blast of wind. "Do you know where you are *now?*"

"Well, that's why I called you back. Not exactly, but everything *is* sort of familiar. I can see a bar and a little grocery store beside the phone booth, and across the street there's this lake or something, with picnic tables on the grass and a few benches here and there. And there's a roof that doesn't have any walls—what do you call it?"

"A pavilion?"

"A pavilion. That's it."

I knew a place just like the one she was describing, a street at the center of town that stretched alongside the park and the reservoir before bending out of sight over a low hill. It couldn't be, I thought. But as I asked her, "What else can you see?" I felt a restless exhilaration making my toes and fingers tighten.

"There's a plane flying overhead. Wait. Two planes. They're both leaving trails in the sky, but they're flying in different directions. One of them is about to hit the other one's vapor trail, right . . . now."

When I looked outside, I saw a white cross above the trees. Two of its strands were unraveling and drifting apart, the other two were blossoming behind pinpricks of silver. "Do they make an X-shape in the sky, Celia? The vapor trails?"

"That's right," she said. "An X."

This would be heaven.

"Stay where you are, honey. I love you. I'll be right there."

"But Dad—" I placed a kiss on the mouthpiece of the Walt Disney Talk-to-Me Telephone and left it swinging from the side of the toy chest.

I snatched the keys from my dresser and drummed downstairs, racing for the front door. Janet was climbing from her car as I stepped outside. When she saw me walking toward her, smiling helplessly, she said, "My word, Christopher, what are you twinkling about?" and I took her hand and pressed it to my cheek, passing my lips over it. Her face slackened in surprise. I let go of her and unlocked my car, and she fastened onto my arm. "Wait, Christopher. There's something I have to tell you."

I slipped into the front seat and started the engine. "Give me twenty minutes," I said. And I backed out of the driveway, racing into town.

I passed a school bus and an automobile trailer and a furniture delivery van. I had to hesitate briefly at a stoplight, but surged ahead at the first break in the traffic, leaving twin strips of black rubber on the asphalt. Our place in the world is the narrowest possible perch—I had learned it many times—and the smallest jostle can cause us to lose our footing. I wanted to get to Celia before she was taken away again. When I reached the reservoir, I parked the car and ran across the street.

There was a phone booth between the bar and the convenience store, a gray metal kiosk with warped glass windows from the waist to the ceiling, and I could see a figure standing inside, her hand resting casually against the door. I shouted to her: "Celia! Celia!"

But it was not my daughter. It was a teenage girl with two long locks of henna in her hair.

I tapped on the glass, and the girl held her index finger out to me—*hold on a second*—and when she opened the booth, cradling the phone against her chest, I asked, "Did you see where—was there someone else here before you? A little girl?"

"I don't know, the phone was just hanging off the hook. Look, can I get back to my conversation, guy?" She blew a strand of hair off her forehead. "I'm kind of in the middle of something here."

I turned away and stood with my hands billed together at my eyes, hunting for Celia along the sidewalk and the green by the reservoir. A man was chaining his bicycle to a fire hydrant, and a mother was wheeling her baby past in a stroller. A few cars were waiting at a stoplight, sending wiry plumes of exhaust into the air. A woman was throwing empty windows of bread crust into the reservoir, feeding either the ducks or the fish, but Celia was nowhere to be found.

When I asked the cashier in the convenience store if she had seen her, she said that she had not. Neither had the bartender in the bar, or the woman tossing bread into the water, or the man locking his bicycle to the fire hydrant. They all knew me or knew who I was, and they looked at me with a pity I had come to recognize.

I walked up and down the block for more than an hour calling her name, but when the sun dropped behind the buildings and the first few sodium lights flickered on, I drove home thinking, You lost her again, you did it, you let her slip away, you son of a bitch.

Janet was waiting for me on the front porch when I pulled into the driveway, a tall glass of iced tea in her lap. She shielded her eyes as the headlights caught her face, then watched me climb from the car and lock the door. I scuffed my way through the grass and sat down beside her, and because I needed to lay my head on her shoulder, I did.

We sat there quietly for a long time, listening to the sawing of the crickets and the occasional bubbling of laughter or applause from our next-door neighbor's television. After a while, Janet ducked her head, tilting forward and twisting around so that she could look me in the eye. "Are you ready to talk now?" she said, and she looked down and slightly to the side, as though she heard a frog croaking by her foot. She rattled the ice in her glass. "I have to—no, it's *important* for me to tell you something."

"About Kimson?" I said. "You don't have to tell me. I already know, Janet."

She sighed and said, "I thought you did." The hood of my car gave off a feeble ticking noise as the heat escaped from the engine. Janet touched her fingers to my neck, tentatively, but pulled them away when a spark of static electricity erupted between us.

We were both surprised. "I didn't do that on purpose," I told her, and she gave a nervous laugh.

My head was still resting on her shoulder, and I could feel the tiny vibrations of her voice rising through her bones and muscles. "Oh, Christopher," she said. "I made a mistake." And as we sat on the porch together she repeated it five, ten, a dozen times, announcing it every few seconds, whenever the silence began to deepen.

I made a mistake, I made a mistake, I made a mistake, I made a mistake.

Which is the explanation for everything.

Love Is a Chain,
Hope Is a Weed

His house, the oldest in the neighborhood, stands below a wooded hillside, so that when he looks out the back window he sees a rising thicket of elm trees, and when he looks out the front window he sees children riding on Big Wheels. Many years after it happened he still lives there. In his side yard the wood thins away to a single elm and a pair of maples, and between their trunks runs a fragment of stone wall, no higher than his knees. The wall was built in the nineteenth century to contain sheep, but the sheep leapt over it during thunderstorms and other bangs of noise and were eaten by wolves. He has read about this in old newspapers. Sometimes he imagines that it is these very sheep, hurdling his wall, that people envision when they're trying to fall asleep. His house is made from the same stone as the wall, a hard yellow stone with rust-red veins that was cut from the Springfield quarry. The quarry is now a cube-shaped lake where teenagers swim and drink beer during the summer. Three of them drowned last year. Because of the color of his house, and the size of its front door, the children in his neighborhood call it the Sand Castle. The world is filled with children. Their Big Wheels sound like rocks tumbling in a barrel.

There is a story about the two maple trees in the side yard of his house that Jim Corrigan, the previous owner, told him before he moved to Florida. Once there were two men—one large, one small—who shared possible paternity for a little girl. Neither man loved the girl, and they would stride past her in the street without a glance, but when her mother died and it was learned that she would inherit the family fortune, they both came to claim their rights as fathers. First the men began to bicker, and then they began to throw punches, and then, right there where those two maple trees grow, the large one and the small one, they drew their pistols for a duel. The girl was watching from her window, and before they could fire, she shouted, "I hate you both!" Whereupon the men were transfigured. This is the story Jim Corrigan told him about the maple trees.

The house is listed in the State Registry of Historic Places, so that he pays no property taxes on it but is required to open its doors to the public one Saturday a month. He tells the people who visit about the winding staircase and the sheep pen and the gravestone in the woods. Sometimes, when the weather is pleasant and the past seems far away, he tells them about the maple trees. Celia used to clamber through the branches of the smaller one, and Janet used to tap the larger one for syrup. When Jim Corrigan finished telling his story, he gave a long sigh and said, "The sand on Fort Walton Beach is as soft as flour, and so are the women."

Todd Paul Taulbee often brings his two Irish setters to fish with him in the pond behind the house. He sits atop a canvas stool on the soft corner of grass below the hillside, casting over the water, while his Irish setters chase each other through the trees. Todd Paul Taulbee has five grown children, all boys, but none of them will fish with him, because it is boring. He and Todd Paul used to chat together occasionally, but though they keep their silence now, Todd Paul continues to fish in his pond. Once or twice a week he will be inside the house reading Trivial Pursuit cards or filling out crossword puzzles and he will hear the beelike sound of a reel unspooling. When he looks out the window, he will see Todd Paul sitting there in the shade by the pond. He wears denim overalls, a baseball cap, and a heavy gray beard. His Irish setters bark at the circles the insects make on the water. They piss against the elm trees. "My sons are all either schoolteachers or vegetarians," Todd Paul told him once, tugging his cap down in a gesture of disgust. "And Tommy, my youngest, is both." There are no true fish in the pond, only tadpoles and minnows. Before Janet left, she used to call it the Puddle. Once, when Celia was only three or four, the three of them—he, Janet, and Celia—caught an eight-pound bass in the Springfield reservoir, carried it home in an ice chest filled with water, and released it into the pond, where it passed like a large white cloud between the reeds. The next day they were hiding on the back deck, watching, when Todd Paul Taulbee hooked it with a #2 fly. He fell off his stool, made a yipping noise, and shouted, "Thank You, Mary, Mother of God!" Celia began to cheer, and then to clap, and then to laugh so hard that she couldn't walk. He had to carry her down to the pond in his arms. In the fall a layer of yellow elm leaves floats on the skin of the water, and in the winter the leaves darken, sink beneath the ice, and turn to a tarry black mud.

He has lived in the house for fourteen years—the seven before it happened and the seven after. The only true sand castles he has ever seen are the kind that skill-less children make on ocean beaches. They look like upside-down buckets, and the first big wave always washes them away. His house looks nothing like a bucket. The front door, however, is twelve feet tall, and as wide as his outstretched arms, and he can see how it might suggest to the children of the neighborhood, in its age and in its stubbornness, a fortress or a castle. Two metal bands cross the door where the wood has split, and it is not hard to imagine it ratcheting down over a moat somewhere. Inside, the light is diluted by the dark wooden walls so that it slants through the windows in sharply defined pickets. He once heard an interview with a German film director who said that houses are like minds: both become unbearable when every corner is filled with light. The director said that he did not know the color of his own eyes. "We must live carefully with ourselves," he said. In the middle of the front room is an old, decorative table with many small kinks and bubbles in the glass. Every year, in late August, between three and four in the afternoon, the light from the front window strikes the table in such a way that its reflection creates a field of stars on the ceiling. He and Janet used to lie on the carpet and wish on them. "I wish I had a million dollars," she would say. And then, later, "I wish it could be the way it used to be." The imperfections in the glass resemble tiny, transparent claws. It is uncanny. Behind the living room, off the kitchen, is a winding staircase which was carved from the trunk of a single giant sycamore tree by the woodwright Edwin Reasoner—born 1830, died 1904. This is what he tells the people who visit his house on the third Saturday of the month, on their Tour of Historic Places. The house itself was built under the direction of stonemason Stephen Wilkes and financed by solicitor Thomas Booth, the original tenant, so that until 1865 it was called the Wilkes-Booth House, and thereafter simply the Booth House. At the head of the winding staircase is the library, and behind that are the morning room and the master bedroom. The closet-sized chamber beside the bathroom, where the Booth family servant once lived, is now used as storage space. And at the end of the corridor, behind the arched window visible from the front lawn, is Celia's bedroom, where she slept for seven years, which he is not yet ready to talk about.

Enid Embry, his neighbor directly across the street, sometimes participates in the historic tours of his home. As often as ten times a year, she will come knocking on his door on the appropriate Saturday morning and say, "Well, it's me again," as he is drinking the last of his instant coffee. "I didn't wake you, did I? You know me, I just can't get enough of this local architecture." She is a lonely woman. The small gift shop she used to operate went bankrupt when a Gift Warehouse the size of a football field opened its doors across town. That very same year, her children moved to Texas and California. Her husband, Hank, retired from the military and promptly died. Every Friday the Gift Warehouse hosts a Treat Yourself to a Gift Sale. Enid Embry believes in flying saucers, and while he conducts her through his house, telling her, once again, about the winding staircase or the coal cellar, she will announce that there was another sighting in Wisconsin last week, or another crop circle in Iowa. She says that the saucers are stealing our children: "They make them swallow this glow-in-the-dark dye," she says, "and then watch them—you know—do their business." She claims that the aliens are in league with the military, though her husband, Hank, would never talk about it while he was alive. Enid Embry leaves a container of beef stew and another of pot roast on his front porch every Wednesday morning. The gesture is supposed to be anonymous, but more than once he has seen her scurrying away from his house as he answers her tap on the door. She dodges between Big Wheels as she crosses the street. She wears bright linen skirts. In every direction, the sky is as blue as powder.

Behind the elms on the wooded hillside, on a table of level ground, is a new Foster's Supermarket. Two years ago there was merely a field of wood char and yellow grass there, and two years before that there was a spinney of oak trees. Springfield has changed so much in the last seven years, he wonders if Celia would even recognize it. He cannot see the supermarket from the window of his house—it is concealed by the hill—but now and then he does spot the wink of a street lamp through the knit of leaves and branches. Once, when he was replacing a pair of cracked shingles, he stood at the very peak of his roof and realized he could see the row of shopping registers and candy racks through the store's plate-glass window, as though he were hovering right there. He felt like a ghost. At night, teenagers steal shopping carts from the parking lot and ride them like carriages over the edge of the hill. They collide with the trees, chipping their teeth, but they do it again and again. All of the carts have mangled frames and trick wheels now, and they weave back and forth through the narrow lanes of the super-market making a mouselike squeaking noise. The manager has posted a sign on the bulletin board reading: ABUSERS OF SHOP-PING CARTS WILL BE FINED AND/OR PROSECUTED. Surround-ing it are all the usual grocery store leaflets: discount shopping inserts, pictures of missing dogs and cats, baby-sitter fliers with a fringe of telephone numbers along the bottom.

———

He has taken to memorizing pieces of trivia. *The giraffe sleeps only half an hour a day. Saint Claire is the patron saint of television. Peter the Great outlawed beards.* Even as a child he had a tenacious memory for such little sparks of information. His seventh grade English teacher, Miss Vinson, once called him an encyclopedia of useless knowledge, a distinction he was young enough to feel flattered by at the time. Recently, though, he has taken up what you might almost call a program of study, reading almanacs, Trivial Pursuit decks, sugar packets, newspapers, dictionaries, magazines, and books with titles like *A Field Guide to Insect Life and Culture* to whittle away from them whatever facts he can. At odd hours of the day or night, with his teeth set and his eyes blinking, after he has set aside his writing, he will find himself rehearsing this particular fact, that particular one known thing. It is like the trick that all children learn of scratching just above or just below a mosquito bite to relieve the itch without inflaming the wound. This is how he explains it to himself: it feels, always, as if he has just been bitten.

On the wooded hillside behind his house, high on the slope, is a single weathered gravestone with two names bitten into the surface: TRAVIS WORLEY, 1917–1925, and beneath it, in smaller letters, BABY GIRL WORLEY, MAY 1925. The gravestone is protected from the heaviest of the winds and rain by a few of the larger elm trees, and the left side is encrusted with rings of bright, pumpkin-colored lichen. On Halloween the kids in the neighborhood swipe the pumpkins from our front porches and smash them against Dumpsters and mailboxes. "It smells like a pie factory out here," Janet used to say as she walked outside on the first of November. The Worley gravestone has been tilted forward by the exposed root of one of the elm trees. A wide bowl of dirt, filled with stagnant water, has formed behind it. In the summer, clouds of mosquitoes hatch from the water and rise wailing into the air. Celia used to call them needle-bugs. Though he has read through the Springfield newspaper archives, searching the obituaries, he has not been able to determine how the Worley children died. *The root structure of a tree, growing unhindered, will be roughly the same shape and size as its branch structure.* This is what happened: his daughter, Celia, vanished seven years ago.

His house has become too big for him—or, if not too big, too encumbered: too freighted or congested or coated with memories. Everywhere he looks he sees pieces of his life with Janet and Celia. In the morning room is the plant he bought the day Celia was born. On the bureau in the library is the chunk of quartz she once carried to kindergarten, telling her best friend, Kristen Lanzetta, it was a diamond. In the living room is the sofa where he and Janet had sex for the last time, on the morning before she left. He pressed his face against her back, kissing the knots of her spine, and she gripped a pillow in one hand—that pillow, there on the easy chair. Afterward, as she wiped the sweat from her face with the bundle of her T-shirt, she said, "I really don't blame you."

"Which means you really do," he answered.

She cocked her head in reflection for a moment. "Which means I really do," she admitted. And then she kissed him on the cheek.

The memories are like millions of tiny ball bearings that send him slipping and tumbling off his feet, making every step precarious. Sometimes he is almost afraid to move. Celia was seven years old when she disappeared and would be fourteen today. Now and then he sees her best friend, Kristen Lanzetta, at the shopping mall. He shops there for pants and sweaters. Kristen and the other girls float down the escalator like mannequins or artist's models, posing meticulously in the glow from the skylights. When they whisper to each other, they move only their heads. Kristen will not answer him when he waves hello to her. He does not know if this is because she is a fourteen-year-old girl and he is an old man, or because she is a fourteen-year-old girl and he is the old man who was the father of her best friend. He does not see himself as an old man—he feels younger, in fact (or maybe it is that the rest of his life, the portion he has yet to live, feels longer), every single morning—but he is certain that Kristen Lanzetta does. Sheila Lanzetta, Kristen's mother, once told him, "You should try not to think about it so much." She is an intelligent woman, an anthropology professor, and she speaks with a note of careful pondering in her voice that makes such things sound reasonable. Sometimes he tells himself this: I do not think about it so much. I do not think about it so much anymore. I really don't think about it so much anymore. But he is unable to believe it. There is so much time to fill.

Ragland Fowler, the Gift Warehouse magnate, has offered to buy his house, but though the ball bearings are everywhere, rolling him this way and that, he is reluctant to sell. What if Celia were to reappear just as suddenly as she vanished, popping through some slit in the air and returning home? How would she ever find him? He can picture her wandering through the house, all the old hallways and bedrooms, and finding them filled with items from the Gift Warehouse—

piñatas, beanbag furniture, Lava lamps with balloons of oil. Everything would be utterly changed. He is afraid to move. He remembers being startled the first time he was paging through the mail and saw her face on a postcard. *Have you seen me?* the card read. CALL 1-800-THE-LOST. And there inside a frame of black lines was Celia. Her photo, the same one he had on the dresser in his bedroom, had been subjected to some sort of aging process, so that her nose and chin were bolder, her hair longer and missing its ribbon. He thought, So this is what you look like now, and was gripped by a sudden fit of shivering.

The mail arrives each day between one-thirty and two, and he often waits on the front porch for it, sipping from a canteen of water. The mail carrier, a French-African immigrant named Nathan Caru, speaks a crisp, night-school English but has a poor ear for the local dialect, which sounds to him, he has said, as if the words were crawling up from underneath the tongue. There is a red, white, and blue stripe across the door of his mail truck that bears a tiny © beneath it. He often points this out to his addressees, expressing amazement. "Who would have thought you could copyright a stripe?" he says. During stuffy weather, when Nathan Caru delivers his mail to him, he offers him a can of soda, during cold weather a mug of hot chocolate. The day he first saw the photograph of Celia on the postcard, he wanted desperately to show it to somebody—to celebrate, or confirm, that it was really there, that she was really his daughter, though even then he knew it was a desperate enterprise. He chased after Nathan Caru as he walked up the block, shouting, "Wait, wait. I have something to show you," and then, when he caught up with him, he presented the card to him. "This is my daughter. Right here in this picture." Nathan Caru smiled his lopsided smile and nodded his head, but it was plain that he did not understand. "Congratulations," he said.

When Celia was four and five and six years old, she had a habit of wandering away. He and Janet would glance up from their reading or their gardening and find that she was no longer in the house, no longer in the yard, and they would wonder where she had drifted off to. *Buster Keaton was given his first name by Harry Houdini, with whom his parents were close personal friends.* Celia would roam through the thicket of elm trees behind the house, collecting the dark, livery mushrooms that grew there. She would step out of her shoes to press her bare feet against the Worley gravestone. She would toss pebbles into the pond, sending clusters of minnows shimmering through the reeds. And she would visit with the nearest neighbors, standing in their driveways as they unloaded sacks of groceries from their cars. In those years this did not seem dangerous. She had never slept a night outside her own bed. The children were riding scooters then, not Big Wheels, and he remembers the sound they made as they glided down the street with their sneakers slapping against the pavement—a sound like a trapped kite knocking against the branches of a tree. Enid Embry, whose husband was still alive at the time, used to invite Celia inside for Kool-Aid and tell her about the aliens. She said they invented Velcro, digital watches, the atom bomb, and nonstick cookware. Sara Cadwallader, who lives two houses down from him, used to let Celia play with her cats, Mudpie and Thisbe. Thisbe had not been spayed, and Mudpie had not been neutered, and they would snake themselves across Celia's legs with a slow, rigid pressure. Once, when he asked Sara about the cats, she told him, *I know, I know, but I just don't have the heart to do it to them. I have to keep my eye on them every single minute of the day.* Greg and Alma Martin, who both teach at Springfield Elementary School, and whose son Oscar was in the same grade as Celia, used to take the two of them to the movies during the summer, and Matt Shuptrine, who lives in the coffee-colored brick house at the end of the block, used to help her chip flakes of crystal from the chunk of calcite in his front yard. The children Celia knew then have graduated from scooters to skateboards, and soon they will graduate from skateboards to cars. He wonders if the children who play in the neighborhood today will graduate eventually from Big Wheels to ATVs—the progression seems inevitable. Though his neighbors have always been kind to him, and though they were always kind to Celia, there are nights when, trying to puzzle it through, he can't help but view them all as suspects.

Every Fourth of July the town hosts a parade that begins at the Courthouse lawn, winds through the business district, and finishes on the banks of the Pinkwater Reservoir. The Pinkwater Reservoir is named not for the tint of the water, which is in fact a healthy greenish-blue, but for Nelson Pinkwater, whose house once stood on the land submerged by the water and who got drunk one night, forgot where he lived, and drove his Dodge Aspen down the shore into the water. Police divers found his car parked on the crumbling strip of his own driveway the next morning. His body was still buckled into the front seat. The parade takes place in the early hours of the evening and is followed by a weenie roast and the launching of the fireworks. Though he no longer attends the fireworks display, he can hear the muffled boom of the charges detonating from his front lawn. When the wind is blowing just right, softly and steadily, he can see the smoke clouds drifting by in the light of the street lamps. Some of the clouds are shaped like palm trees, and some are shaped like tousled hair. He has always found these shapes more interesting than the blossoming red and green sparks of the actual fireworks. The annual Fourth of July parade was instituted in 1974, when Tuck Miller, then mayor of Springfield, marched through town in an Uncle Sam costume, throwing strips of kindled firecrackers onto the curb. A crowd of children gathered behind him, following him to the RESERVOIR COMING SOON sign, where he lit a string of Roman candles and fired them over the swelling water. The next year, when he marched the same route, the children brought their parents and wore costumes and threw firecrackers of their own. Celia was always frightened of loud noises, but she was not afraid of sparklers or whirring dragonflies, and she did like holding the match to the punk. When Tuck Miller turned one hundred years old this year, the *Springfield Citizen-Gazette* ran a photograph of him snapped at last year's parade. He was riding in the sidecar of his grandson Rudy's motorcycle, his Uncle Sam hat yoked atop his head with an elastic chin-strap. His face was twisted together in the wind, and the effect was such that he looked like a tiny child in an enormous hat, indignant and vaguely alarmed. One of the late-night national talk shows broadcast the photograph in a *News of the Week* segment, tagging it with the punch line, *And in this week's Where Are They Now? segment: Captain America and Buffalo Bill Cody.* The audience let fall only the barest smattering of laughter, and afterward the host said, *Come on, folks. Easy Rider? This is top-of-the-line comedy here.*

He has moved the television set into his bedroom, and at night he lies awake in the toneless white light of the talk shows and quiz shows with his pillow folded to a hump beneath his head. He never used to watch TV, and he doesn't particularly enjoy it now, but he uses it like a drug to prolong the last few minutes of the day. After midnight, when he has shut the TV off and the long hours of sleeplessness have set in, he lies in bed listening to the pushing and easing of the wind. The radio tower blinks through the opening in his curtains. He has learned not to stare at the clock, and not to fantasize, and never to reminisce. Instead, he thinks the most mundane thoughts he can and waits for the buzzing feeling of sleep to travel up his body and carry him away. One sheep. Two sheep. Three sheep.

At the west end of town, heaving up between two branches of the state highway, is a rolling field that puts out a blanket of small purple flowers each spring. The flowers are shaped like tiny bells, and they have the sweet, liquory odor of cough syrup. The last time Celia ran a fever, he served her cough medicine from the cap of the elixir bottle. The silver of the teaspoon, she said, hurt her teeth. The field, with its small purple flowers, is displayed on the cover of the local phone book, and on all the Springfield tourism brochures. Eli Butters, the second most prominent town historian, who serves as a criminal court judge, claims that the town derived its name from this field, where the earliest settlers were received by a carpet of purple blossoms in the spring of 1812. Tim Lanzetta, the most prominent town historian, claims that this is a myth—that the town was in fact named for the mineral spring that leapt from the soil behind the old general store, a spring which continued to dribble until the late 1940s, when it was diverted into the lawns of the Valley View subdivision. Janet used to drive through Valley View on her way to Community Orchestra rehearsals. *No valley, no view*, she complained. *Just street after street of dead trees and peeling houses.* She played the clarinet with a beautiful, bleak, pouring-water sound. She twisted like a hooked fish when he kissed the hollows of her knees.

There is a story about the field of purple flowers, which Tommy Taulbee, who teaches English at the local high school, told him once at a school board meeting. Years ago, it seems, when the town was just eight families living in rickety oak cabins, the flowers in the field were as yellow as dandelions. There was a little girl, a blind girl, who liked to go wandering through them, where a wonderful humming noise always filled the air—but where, she wondered, did the humming noise come from? Now and then she would lie on the ground and feel through the grass with her hands, hoping to find it, to touch something that shuddered or twitched or vibrated like a pair of lips. Her father was a careless man, and one day, hunting rabbits in the field, he saw a flash of motion in the grass and fired off a shot. Whereupon he saw his daughter, and his knees foundered beneath him. The next spring the flowers that blossomed in the field were the darkest possible shade of brown, the color of ground coffee, and the year after that they were the color of burnt mahogany. Every year since, they have blossomed a little bit paler than the year before, and one day, fifty or a hundred years from now, they might turn yellow again. It takes a long time for such places to heal. When Tommy Taulbee finished telling his story, he smoothed his beard with his fingers and said, "You know, the day my dad caught that fish in your pond"—and he gave a little breath of laughter—"I just want to tell you, he talks about that all the time. It must be one of the happiest days of his life." Then he turned to him and clasped his arm and said, "You tell your family I said thanks, okay?"

It is the first week of June, and the ladybugs have hatched in multitudes. They boil and hop from the grass, hundreds and thousands of them, so many that he is reminded of the spray from a glass of soda. The spring has been particularly cold this year: the last snow did not fall until April, and there were great dirty hills of it in the parking lots until May. Each season, the ladybugs appear after the snow has melted from the shadiest corners of the woods and the sun has softened the ground. They emerge all at once and migrate slowly to the south, passing from yard to yard as the summer burns on. The television news tracks their progress during the weather report. Shortly after the ladybugs hatch, the neighborhood cats go into estrus, and he can hear Sara Cadwallader shouting at Mudpie and Thisbe from her front porch: *Mudpie! You get down from Thisbe, right now!* Todd Paul Taulbee knocks on his door to ask if it would be all right if he uses the pond for a while. A curtain of fishing lures is hooked to the brim of his baseball cap, and his two Irish setters whirl round and round in the grass. Nathan Caru dons short pants for his mail route, exposing the hair on his legs, which is as thick and snaggy as Brillo. These things happen every year. For two or three weeks, whenever he opens his front door, ladybugs flit into the house, circle around, and bump softly but repeatedly against the windows. He coaxes them into his palm so that he can set them free outside, but he is never able to find them all, and for the rest of the summer their beady red bodies turn up behind the furniture or in the bowls of plants, their legs zigzagging into the air. They are the size and shape of a small split pea, so tiny that they can slip under the door of Celia's bedroom, which remains shut even during the Saturday afternoon tours of his home. *The word formication means the sensation of insects crawling over or under the skin.* At the end of the summer, at the south end of town, the ladybugs vanish, just as they appeared, all at once, burrowing into the ground or folding themselves into the air. No one knows where they go. It is something of a mystery.

For a few weeks every summer, Enid Embry's two grandchildren visit from California. They knock each other down in her front yard, fighting with knee-length socks that have other socks balled in the toes. He can see them from the window of Celia's bedroom: two red-haired boys in cut-off blue jeans whipping their arms about wildly. Celia's bedroom has a dollhouse and a toy shelf and a bed painted to look like a turtle. It has not been changed since the day she left. Once, when Enid Embry came down with a fever, he took her grandchildren swimming in the neighborhood pool, and they quarreled incessantly, about everything, for almost two hours—from who got the red towel and who got the blue towel to which of them was Frick and which of them was Frack. They both wanted the red towel, and, for some reason, they both wanted to be Frick. A jump rope hangs over the doorknob of Celia's bedroom, looped around twice so that it won't slip to the floor. Her bed is painted with the face of a turtle on its headboard, the shell of a turtle on its base, and the four feet of a turtle on its corner posts, so that it looks not only like a turtle, but like a turtle that has tumbled over onto its back and cannot move. For a time, he could smell the dry, floury scent of her skin whenever he stepped into the bedroom, but within a year it faded and was replaced by the smell of rainwater in a metal pail. There is a picture book on her bedside table titled *. . . Is . . .* , illustrated by a Dutch artist named Sisquo. He leafs through it sometimes as he lies on her bed. Each page contains a drawing of a squat little man and woman meant to illustrate some simple catch-phrase, like *Happiness is a sunflower,* or *Love is a rainbow,* or *Sadness is an empty pool.* The catchphrases are all clichés, written according to the same mawkish formula, and in his head he likes to substitute them with adages of his own making—for instance: *Grief is a weight that rolls and rolls, a horrible turning deep inside your body.* Or: *Worry is a mean-faced dwarf who beats on your heart like a kettledrum.* Or: *Regret is the way that ash billows from a fire that has already burnt to embers when you pour water over it in the gray light of the morning.* Celia borrowed the book from her school library, carrying it home on the Friday before she vanished. He did not have the heart to return it. *People reading books blink approximately eighteen times a minute, and they almost always synchronize their blinks with periods, commas, and the ends of lines.* Late in the afternoon, sunlight streams through the arched window of Celia's bedroom, falling across the bed and the carpet. It is the same light that speckles the downstairs ceiling with stars. From this arched window he can see Enid Embry's grandchildren chasing and whipping each other with socks. They play outside all day, but as soon as the sun drops, Enid hurries them inside. "I love having them around, of course, but you and I both know a person can't be too careful these days," she says. Enid traces the sign of the cross on her chest, glancing apprehensively at the sky. A gust of wind hisses through the trees, and every leaf in the neighborhood is moved.

Ragland Fowler, the Gift Warehouse magnate, is running for an open seat on the City Council. He wants to build a strip mall that bisects the entire town, which he says will attract tourism dollars. Opponents are trying to subvert his candidacy by planting FOR SALE BY OWNER signs next to all the RAGLAND FOWLER signs in town. Campaign signs on wooden stakes decorate half the yards in Springfield: DEAN SNYDER FOR ASST. CITY DIRECTOR; RE-ELECT JUDGE ELI BUTTERS; VOTE *NO* ON PROPOSITION 204. Teenagers throw bottles of beer at the signs from the windows of their cars, and at night, on every block, you can hear the blooming sound of breaking glass. One night, while he was reading through the Trivial Pursuit deck, he received a threatening phone call from a person who may or may not have been Ragland Fowler. "I know you're a part of this," the voice said, and it was interrupted by a tick of silence. A long, deep sigh broke through the line. "Hold on," the voice said, "I have another call," and then the connection went dead. Though he continues to reject Ragland Fowler's offer to buy his house, he has neither the will nor the expertise to have participated in the campaign of signs against him. He suspects they are the brainwork of Rudy Miller, former mayor Tuck Miller's grandson, since Tuck Miller, though more than a century old, is also running for the open seat on the city council, and Rudy Miller is working as his campaign manager. Tuck Miller retired from public office in 1978, shortly after the Nelson Pinkwater incident, and devoted himself to the gardening of roses, a hobby he was forced to abandon during the Depression of the 1930s. For the past three years his roses have been ruined by sawflies, and for the three years before that they were ruined by aphids.

He has decided to reenter politics. He is the very model of the age of medication: a life so long that every piece of it has returned.

From the time she was a toddler, Celia's favorite dinner foods were macaroni casserole and a dish called cracker salad that Janet used to make using lettuce, tuna, mayonnaise, and saltines. On those days when he does not find a parcel of beef stew or pot roast waiting by his front door, he spends the afternoon preparing dinner for himself in the kitchen. He cooks better than he eats, and he always has. The refrigerator is filled with neat towers of Tupperware as high as milk bottles. Every few days he scrapes another stack of them into the garbage can. *President Warren G. Harding died in the bathtub, of a busted gut. The word planteration means torture by overfeeding.* Though he can never eat all the food he prepares, he likes the way the smell of cooking spreads from the kitchen while he is at the stove, leaving a thick fog of scent that makes the house feel crowded with family. He and Janet used to make love on the bed and the couch and the bathroom floor, fucking out of eagerness, lust, and affection, and much later out of desperation. Once, when Celia asked them about the thumping noise, they told her there was a badger on the roof.

A few days ago he saw his neighbor Matt Shuptrine at the supermarket atop the hill. Matt clapped his shoulder and asked him, "So what do you think of this weather?" and he did not know how to answer. Instead, he opened and closed his mouth a few times, like a fish, until Matt said, "Well, I've got lightbulbs to buy," and shuffled away, looking back at him queerly. He is less and less able to respond to perfunctory questions, and less and less able to ask them. It is as if the instrument inside him which used to understand how people spoke to one another has cracked and fallen to pieces. He finds it hard to remember which questions are supposed to be casual and which are supposed to be impertinent. He apologizes for all the wrong ones—questions like *How are you doing?* or *What have you been up to lately?*—and he poses the others—*So, are you worried about another miscarriage? Which of your dreams have you given up on for good? What do you two really think of each other?*—with a tone of drowsy half-interest that should infuriate the people he asks them of, but somehow doesn't.

The last time he had sex with Janet, she kissed him and said, "I really don't blame you," and he said, "Which means you really do," and she said, "Which means I really do." The second-to-last time he had sex with Janet, it was purely reflexive, a matter of grief and habit and desperation. They were two people touching and stroking each other because they remembered how and where to touch and stroke each other—that was all. It was as if, together, they were posing one of those perfunctory questions that don't really require an answer, the kind he no longer knows what to say to. The night was warm, and there was a deadness in the air between them, and Janet pushed herself away and began to cry.

"What's wrong?" he asked, though he already knew the answer.

"Why are we doing this?" she said.

Seven years ago, when his daughter Celia vanished, Janet was across town at the Catholic Assembly Hall, rehearsing a Menotti ballet with the Community Orchestra. Sara Cadwallader was outside calling to Mudpie and Thisbe, and the neighborhood children were clattering around on their scooters. Donald and Joan Pytlik were in his living room, where he was showing them the stone fireplace, its alcove darkened from years of soot. *The ashes have left a starlike pattern here on the hearth,* he said, tapping the stone with his knuckles. *Sometimes the wind blows down the chimney, and that pattern you see there is the result.* He looked out the window for a moment onto the side yard of the house. Celia was there, tightrope-walking along the fragment of stone wall between the elm tree and the maples. It was a gleaming spring day, the third Saturday of the month, and there was still a stitch of cold in the air. The sky behind her was a startled blue, so bright that he had to screw his face together to look at her. He cut his eyes away. *Okay, come with me,* he said, and the Pytliks followed him out of the living room. He led them to the kitchen and the anteroom, where he told them the story of Stephen Wilkes and Thomas Booth, and then the story of Abraham Lincoln, and then the story of Edwin Reasoner, the woodwright, who engraved his initials beneath the top stair of the winding staircase. Donald and Joan Pytlik were traveling across the state on a tour of historic yellow stone houses. They wanted to write a book.

It was then that he heard—or thinks that he heard—a shout. It was very brief, almost curt, like the sound that a needle makes when it's lifted too clumsily from a record. The shout did not seem to hold any fear or panic: just a sudden note of surprise. He thinks that he remembers hearing this.

When he passed back through the living room and looked out the window, Celia was no longer there.

The temperature of a raked-out bed of coals is nearly 800° F, but coal conducts heat very slowly, like a sponge, which is why you can walk across it without burning your feet. It was not until later that afternoon that he began to worry. Janet came home from Community Orchestra rehearsal just as the Pytliks were driving away. She stowed her clarinet in the closet and began to read through the entertainment listings in the *Springfield Citizen-Gazette.* They had booked Melanie Sparks to baby-sit that night and were planning to go to dinner and a movie. "Where's Celia?" she asked as she smoothed the creases out of the newspaper. They were sitting by the glass table in the front room— he in the high-backed chair, she kneeling on the floor. It was mid-afternoon, almost four o'clock, and if the sun had been just a little lower in the sky it would have struck the table with its light, throwing the orrery of hidden stars onto the ceiling. But it was not that time of year.

"She's outside somewhere," he said. "Probably playing with some of the other kids."

"As long as she's home by five," said Janet.

"I'm sure she will be." But as the sun tilted toward the trees, and a pale sliver of moon appeared overhead, she was still nowhere to be found. They hollered her name from the four corners of the yard. They searched through the elm trees and behind the Worley gravestone. They walked up and down the block, knocking on all the doors, but they did not find her, and she did not come home. Sometimes he thinks that the world as we know it is as thin as a tissue of cloud—that we can pierce through it without even trying, stepping sideways out of ourselves, and end up in some other world altogether, or in no world at all. Sometimes he thinks that the shout he heard that afternoon was the sound Celia made as the tissue closed behind her. Last month, when he was cleaning the gutter along the roof, he found a red rubber ball she had lost seven years before. It still felt firm between his fingers, and when he tossed it onto the deck, it leapt in a single high arc over the grass and into the pond. When you walk through the doors of the police station, you can hear Kimson Perry, the Springfield police chief, practicing his contrabassoon—a steadfast, plangent, echoing sound that rolls from his office into the marble hallways. That evening, when they could not find Celia, Janet called him at the police station and begged for his help. He said, "Well, normally we're supposed to wait twenty-four hours in a case like this, so we can't file an M.P. form until then. But I'll get some of my men over there and we'll have a look around." He played with her in the Community Orchestra. This was before she left them both behind. Within half an hour, he had arrived with eight of his officers. They coasted noiselessly down the street, their blue lights spinning in the falling darkness, and they *bwooped* their sirens once or twice as they pulled to a stop. Kimson Perry lined his officers up at the rear border of the lawn, six feet apart, so that they looked like golfers at a driving range. "Don't you worry," he said to Janet, just before they stepped into the elm trees. "We'll find your girl for you." And they marched forward on the same beat, the beams of their flashlights cutting across one another like the blades of scissors.

That was the night he began to see flashes of Celia's face where she could not possibly be—in the bank of shadows in his closet, in the torn screen door of the house across the street, in the way a group of twigs were cinched together inside a bush. He would see her from the edge of his vision, and each time he did, something inside him would prickle and let out a gasp before he realized what he was actually looking at. He remembers the day he drove through town and she seemed to explode out at him and disappear a hundred times, to the left and the right, every few seconds, until he thought he was going mad: the police, it turned out, had stapled her picture onto the telephone poles. For a short time after she vanished the police called him every few hours, and later every few days, and later every few weeks. They had interviewed everybody in the neighborhood by then. They had found Donald and Joan Pytlik at a hotel in the northwest corner of the state and taken their statements over the telephone. They had contacted all the area hospitals and runaway shelters, and they suggested that he and Janet continue to call them periodically for any new information. The same phone book that contained the bookstore and locksmith and pizza delivery numbers also contained these other numbers, pages and pages of them, that people turned to only in their grief. He was ashamed to be surprised by this. Soon after Celia disappeared, their neighbors began to arrive at the door with their condolences. They said many things. Thick shocks of grass grow from beneath the fragment of stone wall, sprouting from the crevices he cannot reach with the lawnmower.

Todd Paul Taulbee said, "I'm not much for, you know, the right words, but if I can do anything for you and your family, you just name it. I'm real good with tools, for instance."

Tommy Taulbee, his youngest son, said, "That goes for all of us. The whole family. Anything you need."

Sheila Lanzetta said, "It's only been three days—do you want to hear this?—so you've still got a good chance of recovering her. After a week the chances drop to fifty-fifty, and after that . . ." and her voice trailed away. Kristen Lanzetta, her daughter, who was Celia's best friend, would not leave the car, and she sat in the backseat peeling and reattaching a suction-cup teddy bear to the window.

Enid Embry said, "Sometimes they show up miles away, and they don't have any clothes on, and they don't remember a thing that happened to them until you put them under hypnosis. I've been watching all kinds of stories about it on TV." She gave them a pan of banana bread.

Greg Martin, whose son, Oscar, would be tried four years later in juvenile court for setting fire to the spinney of oak trees atop the hill, said, "We'll be praying for you." His wife, Alma, said, "We already have been."

Ragland Fowler sent a short typed letter that read, in total: "Condolences on the occasion of your loss. Please phone regarding my offer on the house."

Officer Kimson Perry said, "We haven't given up hope yet, and I don't want you folks to, either." He took Janet's hand.

Matt Shuptrine said, "She was a real little trouper, your daughter."

Sara Cadwallader said, "We're all going to miss her."

Melanie Sparks said, "She was the sweetest little kid I knew."

Nathan Caru, who had moved to Springfield only the month before, when Robert Corrigan, the previous mail carrier, retired to follow his brother to Florida, said, "Is there a Celia"—and he mispronounced her last name—"residing at this dwelling?"

Her pictures gradually faded on the telephone poles, were covered by rock-concert leaflets and garage-sale announcements, and finally they were torn down by the Springfield Beautification Committee.

"It was your fault," Janet told him. "You did it."

At seven o'clock exactly, on the night Celia disappeared, there was a rapping on the front door—three quick knocks. The police, who were gathered in his living room, fell suddenly silent, taking root where they stood. Janet flattened a hand to her chest and then motioned for him to answer the door. It was Melanie Sparks. A clutch of police cars was parked behind her, and a pair of headphones hung in a circle around her neck, giving out a tinny heavy metal music. She peered past him into the house. "Are you guys having a party or something?" she said. "I thought I was supposed to baby-sit tonight."

Years later, after his last big fight with Janet, she touched her hand to the back of his neck and said that she did not mean what she had told him. Her skin was cold, and his was warm, and a great snake of shivering traveled up his spine into his shoulders. She said, "I'm sorry, baby. It wasn't your fault. Can you hear me? You didn't do it. You didn't do it, baby. I'm sorry."

In the summer he lets the grass around his house grow as high as his ankles, then mows it into neat parallel bands that look like the nap of a freshly vacuumed carpet. Crickets and grasshoppers hop from his path by the hundreds, along with tiny white insects that look like the seeds of strawberries. Mudpie and Thisbe are fascinated by this turbulence of bugs. They hide behind the fire hydrant and follow the lawnmower with their heads, tripping into the street every time it rattles near. Celia used to straddle the nozzle of the fire hydrant and pretend it was a horse. *Manhattan was purchased by the Dutch from the wrong tribe—the Canarsees, native to Brooklyn, rather than the Weckquaes-*

geeks, who actually lived on the island. In the fall, drifts of elm and maple leaves blow down from the hillside and he rakes them into black plastic trash bags that he stores beneath the back deck. The bags are as large as barrels, and whenever he feels the slumping sensation of gravity that comes just before a heavy rainstorm, he hauls them onto the hill and empties them there. He wants the leaves to sink back into the humus, where they belong. Once, Todd Paul Taulbee saw him walking into the trees with a trash bag saddled over each shoulder and another one hooked to his belt. "What in the holy hell are you doing that for?" he said. The leaves always dry out as soon as the sun comes up, skittering back into the yard in pairs and waves and clusters until the grass is completely hidden. The process never takes more than a week. It is a losing battle.

The children on the block call his house the Sand Castle, and when they see him working in the yard, with his rake and his trash bag and his hair tangled by the wind, they call him the Sand Witch. He can hear them making whooshing noises in the yard across the street as if they are flying about on brooms. Sometimes the bravest ones—ten or eleven years old—will cross the sidewalk and ask him *which* leaves he is raking, or *which* day of the week it is. They always call him "Mister." He pretends not to understand that they are making fun of him, and he has to bottle his own laughter at their bubbling and puffing and coughing. Afterward, he watches them boil back across the street, where their friends wait for them in a cluster. These same children were wearing diapers and pull-ups seven years ago. Some of them were just minnows jerking about in the fish-bowls of their mothers. *The man who developed Vaseline swallowed a spoonful every day and lived to be ninety-six years old.* He once heard an interview with an Iranian film actress who said that she did not lose her virginity, and in fact had never kissed a man, until she was thirty years old. She had been raised to believe that women who allowed their bodies to appear on screen assumed the lust of millions on their souls, and that if they wished to enter Heaven they had to forsake all desire. "People can grow old and ugly from lack of affection," the film actress said. "I was afraid that it would happen to me." In the winter, icicles as round and bulky as legs hang from the eaves of the house, glistening whenever the sun peeks through the clouds. A thick rind of ice covers the Pinkwater Reservoir. Nathan Caru shakes visibly in every limb: he wears a snowsuit as he walks his mail route. In the spring, after the snow melts, the blanket of leaves on the hillside gives off the sweet, slightly acrid smell of burnt marshmallows. When he opens the windows of the house, a bracing wind blows through. He feels like an old man.

Janet called him last week. "I know I don't have the right to say this to you"—and then she said it anyway: "But I do miss you. I wanted to see how you were holding yourself together."

"With glue and paper clips," he told her.

Barely, he meant.

Janet is living with her sister in Chicago. When he dreams about her, she is always riding a glass elevator to the top of a tall building. She steps out and she can see the whole world, highways and cities and a small flickering light on the far horizon, which is his own home, their own home. Though she does not recognize it, she cannot stop looking. When she called that night, he told her that, in truth, he was holding himself together by sleeping and dreaming as much as he could, and, when he was awake, by letting his thoughts snap from subject to subject as though each part of his life were contained in its own little box, shut off from every other. It helps, he has found, to think of his life in this way. Last month, Matt Shuptrine excised the chunk of calcite from his front yard and sold it to the Springfield quarry. He stood with Enid Embry as one of the quarrymen hoisted the stone onto the bed of a trailer and drove it away: it looked like a gigantic human tooth, with a long, tapering root. On Sunday he found the mangled frame of a shopping cart in his backyard with a trail of footprints stumbling away from it into the woods. The footprints looped and slanted over the dewy grass, interrupted by a handprint or two. "From that new supermarket, I guess?" Janet asked him over the telephone, and he said, "Looks like the teenagers finally managed to ride one all the way down." He was standing in the doorway of Celia's bedroom as he spoke to her, the cordless phone held tight in his hand. *You can hypnotize a chicken by holding its beak to a line you've drawn in the sand*. It was night, and the moon shone through the window—a watery yellow color. "Sometimes I think about what it would be like to start over," Janet said.

There is a story about the color of the moon that Sara Cadwallader, who reads picture books to children at the local library, once told him. Long ago, the story goes, the moon was of many different colors, like an opal or a piece of shot silk. On the coldest nights of the year, when the air was so clear you could see to the ends of the sky, the colors seemed to twist around each other like oil on the surface of a puddle. The earth was just a young man then, and he loved the moon like a daughter. Every night he watched her drift through the stars, and when the sun chased her out of the sky in the morning, he opened his other eye, on the opposite side of the world, and watched her once again. It was an act of devotion. One day, though, the earth closed his eyes for a moment, or looked away, or fell asleep—the story is not clear. What is clear is that when he looked for the moon again, she was on the wrong side of the world, falling into the sun. The sky grew so dark above the earth that he could see the stars piercing through like a thousand shining claws. He watched the moon touch the sun, then turn black, and then diminish to the smallest prick. Whereupon she vanished. A few nights later she rose again, but the earth could tell that she was only a ghost, for her eyes were gray and her face was a bloodless white. This is the story of how the moon lost her colors. Now, whenever she shows a brighter face, it is never more than the mistiest shade of yellow, orange, or blue—simply the earth remembering what she used to look like long ago when he was young.

He sometimes stretches out in the grass on the side yard of his house and watches the clouds pass through the branches of the maple trees. In the fall he lies in the leaves, and in the winter on the fragment of stone wall. He can hear the cars on the street, and the birds in the trees, and the children rolling by on their Big Wheels. "The kids don't really like that story," Sara Cadwallader said when she finished telling him about the moon. "With them it's all robots and dinosaurs these days." He knows better than to lie down in the snow. *The human brain runs at a power rating of twenty watts.* He does not have to cook dinner this afternoon, and he will not go inside until it is dark. He will eat a light meal of meat loaf with a boiled egg baked into the center, a little Tupperware casket of which he found waiting on his front porch this morning. He will clean the dishes and lie in bed and watch television until it is time to go to sleep. It is sweeps month, and all the programs will have guest stars. He wishes sometimes that he could find a door that would open into the past, before every single thing that he knows: before Enid Embry lost her husband and Nathan Caru lost his country, before Nelson Pinkwater went dropping through the reservoir like a stone, before Tuck Miller marched through Springfield throwing firecrackers onto the road, before the spring ran dry behind the general store and Travis and Baby Girl Worley died, before UFOs and shopping malls and telephone books and Trivial Pursuit cards.

He would step through the door and there he would be: a century of decades ago, when his house was newly built, the only house in the neighborhood, and flocks of sheep were still cropping the grass. He wonders what the world would look like then. He has heard that the birds were so plentiful the sky went black with wings when they passed. He would like to see that. Why had he imagined that life must always end in death, and never in anything else? He is not nearly at the end.

About the Author

Christopher Brooks is the author of several highly acclaimed works of fantasy and science fiction, including *Songs for Coming Out the Other Side,* winner of the prestigious Peter S. Beagle Award for Short Fiction, and the best-selling Gates of Horn and Ivory trilogy. Born and raised in the town of Springfield, he has lived in the historic Booth House for more than fourteen years, first with his wife and daughter, then with his wife, and now alone. Though he has published a number of essays and articles over the past decade, *The Truth About Celia* is his first full-length book of fiction since 1997.